HAVING A BLAST

The Hardys called their mother from the safe house. "Don't worry, Mom," Joe said. "Frank and I are fine. The smugglers we were after in Mombasa did have an operation here in Stockholm. We broke it up, but we didn't manage to get the one who—"

Joe broke off, wondering if he should tell his mother about the clue he and Frank had found regarding their father's death. Frank shook his head, and took the phone. "We'll see you soon, Mom."

Frank hung up. "I wish—"

His words were cut off by the screeching of tires from the road outside. Joe looked out the window to see a car swerving and a dark figure behind the wheel throwing something stiff-armed.

The living-room window exploded inward as a flat package smashed through the glass to land on the floor.

Frank grabbed his brother's arm. "Get out!" he yelled. "That thing's a bomb!"

Books in THE HARDY BOYS CASEFILES® Series

Available from ARCHWAY Paperbacks

THE PHOENIX EQUATION

FRANKLIN W. DIXON

AN ARCHWAY PAPERBACK
Published by POCKET BOOKS
New York   London   Toronto   Sydney   Tokyo   Singapore

AN ARCHWAY PAPERBACK *Original*

An Archway Paperback published by
POCKET BOOKS, a division of Simon & Schuster Inc.
1230 Avenue of the Americas, New York, NY 10020

ISBN: 0-671-73102-5

First Archway Paperback printing August 1992

10 9 8 7 6 5 4 3 2 1

THE HARDY BOYS, AN ARCHWAY PAPERBACK and colophon are registered trademarks of Simon & Schuster Inc.

THE HARDY BOYS CASEFILES is a trademark of Simon & Schuster Inc.

Cover art by Brian Kotzky

Printed in the U.S.A.

IL 6+

THE PHOENIX EQUATION

Chapter

1

"ONE MAN has been killed here in Stockholm," the grim-faced police officer said to Joe Hardy. "Not to mention your father getting killed in Kenya. We want every detail you've discovered about this smuggling ring."

"You know everything we do about Jumsai Lee Khoo—probably more," Joe snapped back. "Khoo ran arms smuggling here in Stockholm, through a company called Phoenix Enterprises. That sniper you caught shot him to keep us from finding out anything more about their operations.

"As for my father—" Joe fought to keep his square, handsome face expressionless. "He died just as we were closing in on the

African end of Phoenix's animal-smuggling operation."

Joe's struggle wasn't just to hide his grief. He was also trying to conceal the discovery he and his older brother, Frank, had made—they had a small hope that their father was still alive. The clue was just a name on a list they had found hidden in an antiques shop the smugglers had used for a front.

The name was Ezra Collig, chief of police in Bayport, the boys' hometown. Fenton had used his name as an alias in the past. Finding Collig's name could mean that Fenton was still alive and following another arm of the smuggling operation. If that was true, Joe wasn't going to let *anyone* know about it. He had to protect his father and his identity.

He glanced at Frank, whose lean features had tightened into a wary mask. Frank's dark eyes were hooded as he and Joe faced several law-enforcement officials across the table.

Seated at the left on the other side was a high-ranking officer in the dark blue uniform of the Rikspolis, the Swedish national police. Under his carefully trimmed blond hair, his sharp face was angry. His blue eyes were keen as he glared at the boys.

Beside the Swede was a man whose graying hair was styled into a crew cut. Joe recognized the insignia on the collar of his U.S. military uniform as that of Military Police—

2

Criminal Investigation Division. Next came a stern-faced woman in a simple blue suit. She had been introduced to them as a representative from Sweden's national bureau for Interpol. On the far right, also in a suit, was Agent Raymond Fairchild of U.S. Customs.

The forces of law and order may have us outnumbered, Joe thought, but so far we've held our own.

"Agent Fairchild," Frank spoke up, "you can check with your headquarters. Our father took on this case at the request of Congressman Alladyce and Assistant Customs Commissioner Daly. We joined our father as he was closing in on the animal smugglers in Kenya. Then there was that final explosion on the pier at Mombasa. . . ."

"We've told you everything we know about Phoenix Enterprises—both in Kenya and here," Joe added.

"We appreciate the information you've given us," the Swedish police officer said, his English only slightly accented. "But we cannot tolerate any more interference from you. I can understand that you want to get the people who killed your father, but your luck may run out."

Joe stirred, his mask cracking. "Yeah, we were incredibly lucky to find the arms smugglers. How long has Phoenix Enterprises been operating here? You didn't have a clue about what they were doing. We managed to crack this smuggling ring right under your noses."

"You have helped us very much," the blond officer admitted, "although we already had information about Khoo and his partner Karl Bremer."

"What we'd like to know now is where Bremer and Khoo's daughter, Ilsa, disappeared to," Frank said.

"That's what we'd all like to know," the stern-faced Interpol agent said. "My office has assembled intelligence that shows that Bremer may also have been running a network of people smugglers."

She smiled at the Hardys' puzzled looks. "People have many reasons to leave their homeland, and they often end up in your country, the United States."

"If they're heading for America, we should take the lead in this case," the military police officer said. "They were smuggling U.S. military arms and equipment, and now they're probably fleeing toward the U.S."

"The crimes took place in *our* jurisdiction," the Swedish police official pointed out. "We should bring the criminals to justice."

"These crimes are multinational," the Interpol representative added. "While our involvement is basically informational, we are connected with the Rikspolis—"

"I think *my* department should take the

lead," Fairchild said. "Customs and Immigration deals with smuggling both goods and people."

Frank glanced over at Joe. "These people are going to waste more time infighting than trying to nail the bad guys," he whispered. He almost didn't have to lower his voice. The officials on the other side of the table were distracted, arguing among themselves.

In the end the forces of law and order agreed on one thing only. "Your involvement in this investigation is hereby terminated," the gray-haired military police officer told the Hardys.

"Who are you to tell us what to do?" Joe demanded. The officer was obviously not used to having people argue with him.

"Let me put it another way," the blond Swede said. "Twice now you have ruined the plans of this criminal gang. These are dangerous people, and they will want to hurt you. We will keep you under our protection here until the case is finished."

"Keep us out of the way, you mean." Joe could feel the heat rising in his face, but he wouldn't give in to anger. He logically had to convince these unfriendly officials that he and Frank needed to be on this case. Otherwise, they'd never be able to search for their father.

The Hardys did their best, but they might as well have argued with the wall. More Swedish police officers were called into the room, and the boys were marched out, carrying their backpacks.

Their destination turned out to be the garage of police headquarters, where Frank and Joe were turned over to a young police officer. A sprinkle of freckles crossed her cheeks and the bridge of her nose, and her red hair was drawn back in a braid. "Put these on," she said, handing each boy a set of green coveralls, twins of the outfit she herself wore.

"Is this supposed to be a disguise?" Joe asked as he climbed into the baggy green garment.

"It will be, with these." The young officer handed them crash helmets and goggles. "I understand you both can handle motorbikes."

Behind them a door opened and a crowd of young people, all clad in green coveralls, flooded out, pulling on motorcycle helmets.

"It's the shift change for our traffic wardens—meter maids, I think you call them," the young woman said. "We will blend in with them, and you will follow me to your safe house." She pulled on her helmet and gestured for the Hardys to do the same.

"You know," Joe whispered as he tightened his chin strap, "once we're on these bikes, we could be out of here."

Frank shook his head. "Then we'd have

cops as well as the bad guys after us. No, we'll go along—for now."

The boys followed their guide and mounted the bikes she pointed to. Frank revved the throttle. The bike was nothing to attempt an escape on, he decided.

Joe met his brother's eyes and nodded. "These putt-putts are too underpowered," he said, pulling his visor down.

The garage doors rose, and the whine of motorbike engines filled the air as the wardens set off.

"My cycle is number seven eighteen," the young woman said. "Follow me." She joined the rush, and the Hardys trailed her. The swirl of bikes swiftly broke up in the street outside, and the traffic wardens headed off for their beats. The boys followed their guide for nearly a quarter of a mile, turning several corners.

Joe noticed that the young woman kept checking over her shoulder. Apparently she decided they weren't being tailed and gestured for the Hardys to pull up beside a large van.

A pair of police officers stepped out, opening the rear of the van. In moments they had stowed the motorbikes. Frank, Joe, and the young woman climbed into the back as the other officers got in the front. As the van pulled away the young woman unzipped her coverall. Underneath she wore a sweater and jeans.

"I'm Barbro Alvorg," she said. "In a few minutes this van will stop. Enter the green house across the street. That is the safe house."

The van came to a halt, and Barbro opened the doors, jumping down lightly. Frank and Joe followed to find themselves on a narrow, quiet street with boxy, brightly painted houses crowding close to one another.

"Here is the house." Barbro led them across the street. As they went up the short walkway, the door opened to reveal two husky young men. Detectives, Joe guessed, in plain clothes.

"Your duffel bags are here already." A shaggy-haired young detective with a mustache pointed upstairs.

"We put them in your room," the other man, tall and clean-shaven, added as the boys entered the house.

"Nice place—when you finish moving in." Joe glanced around the sparsely furnished living room. There were a couple of graceful wooden chairs and a stark wooden table.

"Scandinavians prefer simple decorations," Frank whispered.

Joe paid little attention, eyeing the futuristic phone sitting on the table instead. "Do you think we could make an international phone call?'' he asked. ''Our mother is in Kenya.''

''Where your father . . .'' Barbro's voice faltered.

The boys nodded.

''We will be in the kitchen.'' The young woman shepherded the two guards to another room.

Picking up the phone, Joe dialed the codes for Mombasa, then the number of the hotel where Mrs. Hardy was staying.

''Mom?'' he said when his call was answered.

''Joe!'' Laura Hardy's voice sounded very far away and very upset. ''Where have you been? I thought you'd call sooner.''

''Don't worry, Mom,'' Joe said. ''Frank and I are fine. The smugglers we were after in Mombasa did have an operation here dealing in U.S. military equipment. We broke it up but didn't manage to get the one who—''

He broke off, wondering if he should tell his mother about the clue he and Frank had found. Was it a good idea to reveal that his father might be alive? The cops assigned to protect them might be eavesdropping.

Frank gave his brother a warning look, shook his head, and took the phone. ''We'll see you soon, Mom.''

Mrs. Hardy drew a tight breath. ''There's no trace of any, of any . . .''

"Mom." Frank's voice got gentler now. "I know this can't be easy for you. We'll be with you to help as soon as possible."

Frank hung up. "I wish—" he began.

His words were cut off by the screeching of tires from the road outside. Joe looked out the window to see a car swerving, a dark figure behind the wheel throwing something stiff-armed.

The living room window exploded inward as a flat package smashed through the glass to land on the floor. Something tinkled inside, and Joe caught a sharp chemical stink.

Frank dropped the phone and grabbed his brother's arm.

"Get out!" he yelled. "That thing is a bomb!"

Chapter

2

PULLING HIS BROTHER ALONG, Frank Hardy dived through the broken window. He and Joe crashed and tumbled into the front garden outside.

A second later whatever glass was left in the window followed them out as the bomb went up. The roar of the explosion was bad enough, but crackling flames rose immediately from the wooden floor and furniture in the room.

"Self-detonating firebomb," Frank gasped, rising to his feet. "A glass vial of one chemical breaks on impact, mixes with another chemical, and the combination goes up."

"Fine—but how do we put it out?" Joe asked, his face pale. "Those three police are inside."

"The local emergency number is 90-000." Frank frowned. "But how can I call for help when I don't know where we are?"

Joe pointed to the other householders, rushing into the streets. "The neighbors will take care of that. We've got to save those cops."

Flames were already dancing in the entrance, so the boys dashed down the narrow passageway between houses to look for another way in. "Here's the kitchen!" Joe yelled, leaping up from the backyard to smash a window.

Oily black smoke rolled out to greet him. Joe staggered back, coughing.

Frank quickly scrambled up and through the opening. "That open window gives the flames a new chimney—they'll head for the kitchen!"

He coughed as he dropped to his hands and knees and crawled along the kitchen floor. The smoke wasn't thick down there. Joe slid in and began choking until Frank dragged him down low.

Frank scanned the room with blurry vision. The smoke had a bitter, chemical smell that attacked his eyes and throat. But he could make out the clean-shaven detective pushing himself up to his knees. The shaggy guard and Barbro were still on the floor, passed out.

"They must have been closer to the blast," Joe said, lifting up Barbro. Frank and the clean-shaven man helped the other detective to his feet.

They bundled the officers out the window as the kitchen door blazed up. Frank and Joe bailed out a second later before tongues of flame started licking at the window frame.

"That fire's too close," Frank gasped. "We've got to get them around to the street."

Coughing and choking, Joe carried Barbro to a neighbor's lawn. He performed mouth-to-mouth resuscitation on her while the clean-shaven officer tended to his partner.

Frank waited until Joe pulled back for a moment. Then Frank knelt down and spoke to his brother in a low voice. "This whole safe-house thing was supposed to be secret. They even went through that traffic warden stunt to confuse anybody who might be staking us out. Barbro was sure nobody had followed us."

Joe's eyebrows rose. "So how did anyone know where to throw that firebomb?"

Frank nodded grimly. "Too many times, the smugglers have known where we were— or what we were doing. Back in Africa Martin Jellicoe was supposed to be working for customs. Instead, he was in the bad guys' pockets, feeding them information."

"We know the ring is big business," Joe admitted. "Maybe they've got more officials on the payroll than Jellicoe." He glanced at Frank. "So what do we do?"

"I think our first move is to disappear," Frank said. "At least then nobody knows where we are."

Joe watched as the top floor of their supposed safe house collapsed in flames. "Our bags were in there. We'll be running with just the clothes on our backs."

"At least we've got our money belts and passports," Frank added, with a wary glance down at Barbro. The young woman was coughing now but was still dazed. "How is she?"

"She'll make it—no need for us to hang around," Joe said.

Frank led the way, rising quietly and fading back into the crowd that surrounded the disaster site. The one police officer who might have stopped them was still kneeling over the other downed guard. In the distance Frank heard the two-toned call of European sirens approaching. Soon ambulances, fire fighters, and police would arrive. The time to disappear was now.

A shout rang out as the police guard realized he had lost sight of his two charges. By then Frank and Joe had reached the back of the crowd. They set off at a steady pace down the block.

"Not too fast," Frank warned in an undertone. "We don't want to call attention to ourselves."

An ambulance accompanied by a police squad car roared past them. By the time they arrived at the burning house, Frank and Joe were out of the neighborhood.

"Okay, we got out of there," Joe said as they headed down a side street. "Our next step is to find out if Dad is really alive. Then we'd better catch up with Ilsa Khoo."

"Which means tapping into Karl Bremer's people-smuggling operation," Frank said. "We know that if Dad's alive, he must be somewhere in that pipeline. And if Bremer and Ilsa wanted out of town, my guess is they'd use one of their ring's established routes."

"So we have to tap into that network somehow," Joe agreed. "Any ideas?"

Frank frowned. "Unless we want to question everybody in Stockholm, I suggest we pay another visit to Mr. Bremer's place."

"That place may be crawling with cops," Joe objected, then shrugged. "I know. That's a risk we'll just have to take."

They reached a main road, one Frank recognized from his tourist map, and then headed for the nearest *tunnelbana* station. A short ride later they emerged from the subway station in Stockholm's city center.

"As I remember, Bremer's shop is this way," Joe said. He moved along the crowded city streets until they came to a less-busy area. On a quiet block they found the four-story building with the shop on the ground floor. Joe scanned the living area above. "No lights on—nobody's home."

Frank walked up to the length of tape that sealed the door. He pulled the tape aside and ran an eye down the street to see if anyone had noticed them. No one was moving along the side street.

"We're in luck," he said, pulling a lock-pick tool from a pocket. "When we chased Jumsai Khoo here last night, we kicked the door in. This replacement lock they installed is a joke." After a moment's work the door swung open.

The Hardys stepped inside cautiously. The last time they'd entered this shop they'd been hot on the trail of Jumsai Khoo and his daughter, Ilsa. Since then the shop office had been seriously gone over by the police. The hidden panel Karl Bremer had opened was empty, obviously searched by police specialists. Drawers were missing from the desk and from several file cabinets.

"Looks like we're a little late," Joe said. "Everything here must have been carted downtown as evidence."

"Not everything." Frank stood in front of a large computer setup. The keyboard and monitor screen were on top of the desk, but the big, boxy central processing unit—the "brains" of the computer—stood up like a small tower from the floor.

"It's bolted in place," Joe said.

"Yeah. And while Bremer might have dealt in antiques, he sure didn't keep his records on one. This baby is so hot, it's almost next-generation."

Before he could move to examine the machine, they heard a rattle from the rear of the store. The boys ducked behind a faded tapestry that hung down one wall.

They took cover just in time. No sooner were they hidden than they heard stealthy footsteps moving along the wooden floors. Frank looked at Joe. There was no reason for a police searcher to come in a back door.

Frank found a worn place in the tapestry, just at eye level. He couldn't see the whole room, but he did have a clear view of the desk and the computer screen and keyboard, barely two yards away.

Then a man stepped into his field of vision. The intruder was pale and skinny, all knees and elbows. His dirty-blond hair was stringy and unkempt and hung down as he bent over the keyboard.

In a moment the computer screen blazed with light as the man turned the machine on. He tapped slowly on the keyboard, hunting for the letters. Frank frowned. He recognized the word on the screen for checking computer functions. It was in English. The machine was programmed in English, probably because so many Swedes spoke the language. Frank had used this program himself many times.

But the familiar program menu didn't appear. Instead a list of names flashed on the screen. Bremer must have hidden the information under a dummy file name!

Frank squinted, trying to make out anything on the list. A short line caught his attention— LEA KERK.

Then the names abruptly disappeared, and the intruder began another stint of hunt-and-peck typing. The words DELETE ALL? appeared on the screen.

Frank burst from concealment as the skinny man's finger found Y for yes, then hovered over the return key.

If he pressed that button, an important clue would be wiped away!

Chapter

3

FRANK HURLED HIMSELF at the skinny man in front of the computer, flinging aside the tapestry he'd been hiding behind. The wooden rings that held up the heavy cloth clacked together, and the intruder whirled around.

Even as the man moved his finger stabbed down. Frank saw the screen go blank.

It's erasing, Frank thought. All the files will be lost. He hesitated, torn between the intruder and the computer.

The trespasser's foot lashed out at Frank's chest to send him tumbling backward. That guy may be skinny, Frank thought, but he packs a nasty kick.

Joe burst from cover an instant after Frank, but he was two steps behind the intruder as the man whipped around and dashed from the room. By the time Frank got back on his feet, both had disappeared. He heard a door slam in the distance.

Frank stepped back to the computer. It looked as if an entire directory had been deleted. He searched the hard disk and finally found a file restoration program.

"You can do it," he muttered, setting the program to work on the deleted directory. "Yeah, here it is." The mysterious list was back on-screen in glowing letters.

"It's the same list, all right. There's that short name—Lea Kerk." Frank's fingers flashed across the keyboard, and he turned on the printer. Moments later he had a copy of the list in his hand.

Joe returned, shaking his head. "I wish we had a guy like that on our track team."

Joe was cut off by the sound of onrushing two-tone sirens.

"Guess somebody in the neighborhood noticed us or our new pal," Frank said. "Let's get out of here."

He glanced at the screen. "I think I'll leave this for the local law. With a small change." Frank deleted Lea Kerk's name. "Let's have one thing up on the boys in blue."

They went out the back door, and Joe showed Frank the route the intruder had used to escape.

"I think our next stop should be the offices of Phoenix Enterprises."

Joe stared at his brother. "Sure. I bet they'll be pleased as anything to see us, after we blew another of their operations."

"Not everybody at Phoenix is a crook," Frank pointed out. "Eleonora Grunewald isn't. Jumsai Khoo used her and her name for respectability in his smuggling operation. She'll help us find out if any of the people on our list are associates of Khoo's."

The Phoenix offices were in the rear of the riverfront warehouse in central Stockholm. As Frank had guessed, the place was in total chaos after the announcement of the latest scandal. Getting past the receptionist was no problem. She was overloaded, dealing with an avalanche of calls and an onrush of reporters. The Hardys entered Eleonora Grunewald's office to find her sitting behind a sleek Scandinavian-style desk, talking on the telephone.

"I wish I could be certain that it's as much of a shock to you as you say, Mr. Banner," the handsome blond woman said into the phone. "It was certainly a shock to me to discover that criminal elements were using Phoenix Enterprises for their own purposes. We are, of course, giving the authorities every assistance in their investigations. Yes, I thought you would agree. Yes, Lyle. I'll keep you updated on the situation."

"Is that Lyle Banner, the American end of the Phoenix organization?" Frank asked.

Grunewald hung up and smiled at the Hardys. "What are you doing here?"

Frank noticed that Eleonora Grunewald was as elegantly dressed as ever. She also seemed to have aged about ten years. The skin on her aristocratic face sagged now, and there were dark smudges under her eyes. Frank knew she had good reason to look so bad—she'd almost been murdered the night before.

"We're looking for help in hunting down Khoo's daughter and Karl Bremer. I've got a list of people who may be doing business with Bremer, and I want to know if Khoo dealt with any of them."

"That's really a matter for the police," Grunewald began.

"The police aren't the ones who saved you last night," Joe pointed out simply. "We were."

The woman took a deep breath and nodded. "Mr. Khoo kept the smuggling end of our business to himself, as I discovered so disastrously. But you may check his office."

She went to a heavy wooden door in a side wall and swung it open, revealing another office. "The police have already been inside, but it hasn't been sealed. There are still things they want to move out."

Jumsai Khoo's office was the complete opposite of Eleonora Grunewald's sleek, bare chamber. Papers were piled on the surface of every countertop and table.

"Looks like you're inheriting a mess in more ways than one," Joe told the aristocratic woman.

Eleonora Grunewald had the grace to look embarrassed. "I have a lot to learn," she confessed. "Now, Jumsai had one of those circular files."

Frank stepped to the rolling card file on Khoo's desk and began flipping through the cards on the Rolodex. At the beginning of the Ks he found a card for Kerk Travel, listing Lea Kerk as the owner. "We just got one match from our list," he said.

He was interrupted by the buzz of the intercom on Eleonora Grunewald's desk next door. "Ms. Grunewald," the harassed voice of the receptionist called through, "more police on their way to see you. They won't—"

"Go and talk to them," Frank said in a low voice. "We'll stay in here."

Eleonora Grunewald returned to her office to wait for the police, closing the connecting door.

"Ms. Grunewald?" Joe and Frank recognized the voice speaking on the other side of the panel. "I'm Raymond Fairchild of U.S. Customs, and this is Ina Magnusen of Interpol."

"Come on," Frank whispered to Joe. "We're out of here."

Joe flipped the Rolodex to a new card and followed his brother out.

When they reached the street Frank again consulted his map. "What do you know? Lea Kerk's office is near here. Suppose we go and check it out."

A short walk from where they were, the travel agency turned out to be a storefront on a small, winding street. "Is this it?" Joe asked, nodding to a restrained sign that simply read, Kerks.

"That's the way Swedish indicates a possessive," Frank explained. "We'd have an apostrophe in there, but this is definitely Lea Kerk's place. Look at the posters inside: *turist* and *resa*, that's Swedish for tourist and travel. Let's find a good spot to stake the place out."

"Got it!" Joe was already moving down the block. Frank followed him to a street kiosk where a man was selling hot dogs.

"Med brod och senap," Joe was telling the man as Frank caught up. Joe grinned at his older brother. "See, I've learned some Swedish. If you don't ask for bread and mustard, you just get a naked hot dog."

As Joe paid, Frank smiled to see two wieners being handed over, each of them surrounded by rye bread and topped with spicy mustard.

The kiosk provided a perfect observation post. As the boys slowly consumed their hot dogs they saw several people enter and leave the travel agency.

"This reminds me of the game we used to play in airports when we were kids," Joe whispered to Frank. "Guessing what travelers do for a living."

A dark-skinned man with blunt features and a heavy black mustache moved warily up to the travel agency.

"That one's easy," Joe said. "He's an Arab terrorist."

Frank laughed. "I'd guess he's Turkish. A lot of Turks have come to northern Europe, looking for work."

A few moments later the man hurried out of the store. Then came a pinch-faced man in a wrinkled trench coat. Thinning hair was pulled across his pale scalp, and the man's watery blue eyes darted around suspiciously before he entered the shop.

"The guy's obviously a spy," Joe stated.

"He did look awfully worried for someone arranging simple travel plans," Frank admitted.

"I hope *I* never get stuck on a tour with someone like that," Joe murmured.

The street was quiet for a while, and the

boys bought a couple more hot dogs. Then a young couple hesitantly made their way down the sidewalk. In one hand the young man carried a piece of paper, which he peered at while checking addresses. The couple found their destination and scurried into the travel agency, clinging to each other like frightened children.

"No kidding around this time," Frank said. "They look exactly like refugees."

Joe nodded, his face serious. "Well, I'd say Lea Kerk has some interesting clients."

"And I'd say we've had enough hot dogs," Frank added. "We've got to figure a way to get to Lea Kerk."

"I think we need more than that," Joe objected grimly. "One of us actually has to infiltrate the people-smuggling operation."

"Let me guess who's volunteering," Frank inquired in his most sarcastic tone. "Are you nuts? That has to be the most—"

Joe raised a hand to cut off his brother's protests. "Sure it's dangerous, but whoever really runs Phoenix keeps the various operations separate. I've got the perfect way to win Ms. Kerk's confidence and get in good with her." He smiled at Frank. "And you get to play a very important part."

It was evening but still light when Lea Kerk finally closed her travel agency. The boys had a hard time adjusting to the approximately twenty hours of light each day in the summer. Lea had locked her shop door and was walking down the street when she heard the rapid slap of running footsteps behind her.

She turned to see a young, dark-haired man come around a curve in the road. He turned a frightened face over his shoulder.

A second later she saw why. The runner was being pursued by another young man, blond and tough-looking in a torn T-shirt. He carried a length of metal pipe.

Before she could even call out, the blond roughneck had tackled the other boy. They rolled behind a car, and Lea saw the pipe rise up, then come down with a sickening smash.

The blond boy stood up, a crumpled fistful of kronor bills in his left hand. His right still held the pipe, one end now dripping red. It was obvious that the other boy wasn't getting up.

"Why did you run if you didn't have any cash?" the young bandit muttered as he jammed the money into his jeans pocket. "You went and got yourself killed for nothing."

He turned from the body Lea Kerk couldn't see, and his hard blue eyes focused on her as she stood frozen by her car.

"Great. A witness." Still hefting the deadly pipe, the young man came at her.

Lea Kerk opened her mouth to scream and instead got rammed against her car. As she tried to catch her breath a hand tore the car keys out of her grip.

"Or maybe a getaway?" The blond boy unlocked the car door and shoved her inside. "You know this town, so you should know how to drive me out of it." He looked from the car keys in one hand to the bloodstained pipe in the other.

"Drive," he said, "or die."

28

Chapter

4

EVEN AS LEA KERK'S CAR pulled away the victim of the attack was rising from behind the parked car that had hidden his death agony. Frank Hardy grinned at the melon he'd been carrying in a paper bag. Now the fruit lay smashed in the gutter. Joe had been right to insist on buying it. The sound effect when he'd hit it with the pipe had been very effective.

Frank scooped up the ruined fruit and tossed it in a trash bin, along with the packet of fake blood he'd been holding. Some had gotten onto the pipe. He'd held the rest as a backup measure, in case Lea Kerk stepped forward to view the crime. Now as he sprinted around the corner Frank was glad that hadn't happened. He would have a tough job hailing a taxi covered in blood.

A local cabbie saw his frantic hand-waving and pulled up.

"It's my girlfriend," Frank said in an agitated voice. "I knew she was going out with somebody else, and now I can prove it. They just left in a gray Volvo."

More than a little amused, the cabdriver responded to Frank's directions to "follow that car." Frank sank back in his seat. He hoped the chase wouldn't be too long. Swedish cab rates were tremendously expensive.

She's certainly buying my bad-boy impersonation, Joe thought as he watched the expression on Lea Kerk's face. She nearly jumped out of her skin when I told her to take me to her house.

Now the travel agent sat huddled on the couch in her living room, staring at Joe with fearful eyes.

"My luck's been lousy since I left the U.S.," Joe said, pacing around the room. He gave the woman a hard look. "Like tonight. Understand what I mean?"

Lea Kerk shrank deeper into the sofa cushions.

"See, I got connections," Joe went on, boasting. "I work for some of the biggest guys in the States. They got me out of the country when the cops were threatening to take me in for questioning."

Joe strutted a little. "Yeah, the big shots back home think I got potential."

Then he frowned. "But the guy they set me up with over here got himself arrested, and now I got no money, no papers, and nowhere to go."

A gleam of hope appeared in Lea Kerk's eyes. "Where would you like to go?" she asked.

"Home," Joe said bluntly. "I don't like this Europe jazz. People don't talk American. Well, most of you squareheads—I mean, Swedes—do, but it still ain't home."

"Suppose I could get you there," Kerk said, trying a desperate smile. "After all, I am a travel agent—"

"Yeah, I'm real sure you could get me a passport out of thin air," Joe cut her off. "Get the wax out of your ears, lady. I got no papers."

"I know people who can fix that," Lea Kerk said desperately. She licked her lips. "You may be surprised, but I have a connection to a good operation that makes the kind of, ah, travel arrangements that you need."

No fooling, Joe thought.

"They know what they're doing," she went on nervously. "Believe me, you could be out of this country like *that!*'' She snapped her fingers. "What do you say?"

"I say I never heard of people smugglers who took charity cases," Joe said. But he let a little hope and curiosity show in his face. "Of course, there are guys back in the States who would pay my freight. Fat Abie Mandelbaum, for instance—"

"I'm sure something could be worked out," Lea Kerk said eagerly. "Let me make some phone calls."

She dialed a number and shuddered as Joe grabbed the phone so he could listen, too.

"This is Lea Kerk," she said in English so Joe could understand. "I have a—client."

The only answer from the other side was a grunt. Then a heavily accented voice said, "So when do you start to recruit?"

"This person needs to, ah, *travel* as soon as possible," Kerk said. "There will be money waiting on the other side."

Another grunt from the other end of the phone. "I tell Ducats, he decides what to do." There was silence, and Joe almost believed the grunter had hung up. Abruptly, the gruff voice was back on the line. "Where are you now?"

"We're at my house," Lea Kerk said. She cast another nervous glance at Joe. "Could you please tell him to come soon?"

"Sure. He come soon," the mysterious voice said.

The line went dead.

Joe hung up the extension. "Well, they seemed to pick up on what you were saying," he said. "Maybe this smuggling gig is exactly what you said it is."

He flung himself down on the couch, making Lea Kerk jump. "So how soon is soon? I mean, I know you sq—uh, Swedes—are on the ball."

Lea Kerk looked a little confused. "Mr. Ducats is not Swedish," she said. "I don't know what country he is from." She winced as Joe swung his feet onto her coffee table and set them down with a loud crack.

Outside the suburban Stockholm house, Frank Hardy scanned the neighborhood. He had asked the cabdriver to drop him on the corner of the block, not wanting to follow Lea Kerk's car too closely. While paying his fare he memorized the house that Lea Kerk and Joe entered.

"Good luck," the cabdriver said as he pulled away.

It hadn't been easy to keep the house under surveillance. The neighborhood was too open, the streets full of houses. There were no convenient hot dog stands to hide behind.

I'm going to stick out like a sore thumb just standing on the sidewalk, Frank thought.

He started walking around the block. If Lea Kerk's street is empty on my next pass, I'll take a chance on getting around the back of her house, Frank decided.

Strolling around the block, Frank did his best to act nonchalant. As he passed the drive of Lea Kerk's house he dived behind the low stone fence that separated her front lawn from the sidewalk.

Now to work my way around the house, Frank thought. He used the garden wall as cover all the way to the rear of the house.

Frank peered through a lit window and found that he'd placed himself at the corner of the living room. Lea Kerk and Joe both sat on the couch. The travel agent was giving Joe dirty looks, probably because Joe had his big feet resting on her coffee table.

They sat in silence. Sure, Frank thought, neither can be in the mood for small talk. Lea thinks Joe is a killer, and Joe must be nervous, trying this crazy charade.

Frank heard the sounds of a car slowly moving down the street, then stopping. He took a quick look around to the front of the house. An expensive sedan had pulled into the drive.

By the time Frank got back to his vantage point, the doorbell had already rung. Lea

Kerk went to answer the door, with Joe standing behind her.

Two men came into the house. One was short with a dark complexion. His expensive designer suit was stretched over his slightly tubby frame. The other was tall, blond, and burly and was wearing a black leather jacket.

Frank recognized the types immediately. A boss and his bodyguard, he said to himself.

Joe strode cockily up to the smaller, well-dressed man. "You the guys who are going to help me? Pleased to meetcha. I'm Joey Tate."

He extended his hand to shake, but the small man stepped away. The big bruiser moved into his place and stiff-armed Joe.

The unexpected impact knocked Joe off balance. He stumbled, and the smaller man's leg came up behind him.

Frank bit his lip as Joe landed flat on his back, lying stunned for a second.

That second was all the big bruiser needed. His hand darted into his jacket and reappeared with an automatic pistol.

Frank froze.

The muzzle was pointed right at Joe's head!

Chapter

5

JOE HARDY FROZE on the floor, staring up the barrel of a loaded pistol. The mouth of the gun looked about as big as a water main. "Wha-what's going on?" he finally managed.

"A small security precaution," the short, round-faced man in the expensive suit said. "If you would be so good as to roll onto your stomach."

The big guy with the gun edged a toe under Joe's rib cage, flipping him over. With a gun pointed at his head, Joe offered no resistance. At least the goon hasn't pulled the trigger, he thought. Yet.

"Hands clasped and behind your neck," the little man said.

Joe complied, and the big man frisked him

with one hand. As he patted down Joe's waist he spoke for the first time. "Money belt."

The smaller man waited until the bodyguard had completed his search. "Now, young man, you will bring out that hidden belt slowly and carefully, if you value your life."

Joe did as he was told, keeping his hands in sight at all times as he took the money belt from under his clothes.

"Give it to me. No, toss it over," the plump man ordered. He caught the money belt in midair, unzipped it, and examined the contents. "No passport, and only a few American dollars."

Joe gave an inward sigh of relief. He'd been right to give Frank his passport and most of his money. "That's what I told the broad here." He tried hard to make his voice sound tough, which wasn't easy.

"That is what he said," Lea Kerk admitted. She went on to give the rest of Joe's story.

"Well, Mr. Tate," the short man said, using the alias Joe had chosen, "you can call me Mr. Ducats. And I trust you have learned the first lesson of our business association. I am the boss, and *you* have just become cargo."

Ducats gestured to his bodyguard, who holstered his gun. Joe warily got to his feet.

"Cargo does not make trouble," Ducats went on. "It does exactly what it is told to do. In return, we furnish travel money, all the necessary papers, and safe passage to the United States. Your friends in America will pay us ten thousand dollars. This is possible, yes?''

"Sure," Joe said, trying to sound as confident as possible. "Big Abe's good for it."

"Excellent," Mr. Ducats said. "Because if you are not worth ten thousand dollars to my organization, your life is then worth the price of a single bullet."

The gun suddenly reappeared in the big bodyguard's hand.

"You understand?" Mr. Ducats asked in a silky voice.

"Right. I understand. You got my word on it. And when Joey Tate gives his word—''

Ducats cut him off. "I understand from Ms. Kerk that you have no luggage. So there is nothing to keep you here."

Joe shrugged. "Guess not."

"You will spend the rest of tonight in one of our houses and begin your journey tomorrow morning."

"Just come with you?" Joe asked, trying to stall for time. I hope Frank has arranged some way to follow me, he thought.

"For everyone's safety, including your own," Mr. Ducats said, "you will not be out of our sight."

The big bodyguard's hand was under his

jacket again. Joe knew when to give up. "Let's go."

Outside, Frank Hardy was already dashing down the block, desperate for a cab. There wasn't one to be found in the quiet neighborhood.

Frank hid behind a tree, checking back toward Lea Kerk's house. The small man in the suit led the way out of the house. Then came Joe, with the burly bodyguard close behind.

Lea Kerk did not see them off. Even from where he was hiding Frank could hear her door slam.

Joe slid into the backseat of the luxury sedan with Ducats, and the guard got in behind the wheel.

Come up with something quick, Frank told himself, or Joe will roll right out of your life—and maybe out of his.

Frank needed wheels. And where was he going to find them?

Then his eye fell on Lea Kerk's gray Volvo, parked in her drive. A moment later Frank was across the street and behind the wheel. He released the parking brake and let the car roll silently down to the street.

Frank hot-wired the ignition and took off in pursuit of his brother. Maybe I should feel bad about this, he thought. But somehow, I don't. If Lea Kerk is in league with these lowlifes, the least she can do is help me keep Joe alive.

He had some nerve-racking minutes, staying close to the sedan until it got on the highway back to Stockholm. Once on the highway, Frank was able to fall back in the flow of traffic until the smugglers' car took an exit. Frank followed the car into a neighborhood where expensive sedans normally didn't go. He felt conspicuous enough in a Volvo.

He saw Mr. Ducats's car come to a stop in front of a seedy apartment house. Joe and the gorilla got out, and the short boss drove on. Frank brought his car to a stop by the doorway. The bodyguard was pressing the lowest button on the intercom to get inside.

As Frank drove on he thought, Okay, I know where they'll be all night. Now if only I can find a safe place to leave this car . . .

Inside the building the burly bodyguard prodded Joe up four flights of stairs. Just my luck, Joe thought as they walked down a dingy hallway. The first step of my great getaway is to climb to a fourth-floor walkup.

Down the hall a scarred wooden door swung open to reveal another burly type, dark instead of blond like Joe's shadow, with a scar running the length of his face. He stood silent as they walked into the apartment. Joe noticed that the man's other hand, the one that had been hidden behind the door, held a naked automatic.

"So, Nils," the armed guard said to Joe's warder. Strong white teeth gleamed against the dark stubble on his lower face. "Another one, eh? Soon we have no room at the inn."

Nils pushed Joe down a short hall and into the living room. Several people were there already. Joe recognized some from the stakeout at Lea Kerk's. There was the intense-looking swarthy-skinned man. In the corner was the frightened couple. Slouched on a stained couch was the tight-faced pale man. The rest of the inhabitants were burly, hard types. More guards, Joe guessed.

"Go in. Sit," Nils said.

The only open seat was beside the pale man. For a moment the man's face relaxed its usual glare. "Good," he said, although it sounded more like "goot" with his German accent. "At least I have some decent company on this trip."

He glanced at the others in the room. "A white man."

Joe jumped up. "That line of garbage went out long ago."

His sudden movement made the guards turn. "I don't mind the stains on the couch," Joe told them. "But I can't stand the smell."

He walked over to the young couple, who stared at him with almond-shaped eyes. "I'm

Joey Tate," he told them. "Looks like we're going to spend some time together."

"Cheng Wong." The young man gestured to the woman with him. "My wife, Lu. She speaks not much English."

"Good to meet you," Joe said.

After a few minutes of broken conversation Joe headed over to the other man.

"Fuat Dere, once of Turkey, soon to become an American, I hope," the young man introduced himself. His English was better than the Wongs'. "I see you've made friends with everyone—including the delightful Gustav Strular."

"The great white hope, you mean?" Joe asked.

"The East German," Fuat Dere said.

"You're a little behind the times," Joe told him. "There is no East Germany anymore."

"But there are still lots of East Germans," Dere told him. "You can tell by the accent."

"And how does a guy from Turkey know about German accents?" Joe wanted to know.

Fuat Dere laughed harshly. "Times are very hard in my country. My family has been over half of Europe looking for work. Me, I passed through Germany. That man speaks with a Prussian accent, and Prussia's in what used to be East Germany."

"What has that got to do—" Joe stopped

when he heard the apartment door open again. He looked down the hall—and froze.

Joe had seen that dirty blond hair, that lanky form before. It had been at Karl Bremer's. This was the guy who'd tried to erase the computer files. Now the man carried a bulging satchel.

The big question is, did the guy see me at Bremer's? Joe thought. If he did, it means my cover's blown—and I'll be blown away!

Then a door swung open halfway down the hallway, and one of the security people yelled, "Hey, Klaus! Come in here!"

The newcomer turned back.

Fuat Dere smiled cynically, watching the look on Joe's face. "Welcome to the world of illegal aliens, my friend. Wherever you are, whenever a door opens, you have a moment of fear."

Joe managed to give the young Turk a shaky grin. Then he noticed that Gustav Strular's watery blue eyes had missed nothing of his reaction.

That guy is going to be trouble before this little class outing is over, Joe thought. Major-league trouble. My only hope is that I catch up with Dad before Strular tries anything.

Frank Hardy sat behind the wheel of Lea Kerk's car, planning his next move.

If I'm going to follow Joe and offer effective

backup, I need equipment, he thought. At the very least I need a radio tracker. Some long-range listening equipment would come in handy as well. I can't stay as close to Joe as I have without calling attention to him—and to me.

Frank's problem was that the equipment he needed would cost a small fortune—and he wasn't even sure that he could find it on the open market.

It was the sort of stuff law-enforcement agencies had on hand, Frank knew. But all the forces of law and order were against them just now. He couldn't try to get it without being arrested or detained again. Then Fenton Hardy would have no backup.

So I can't buy the stuff, and I can't get it from the cops, he concluded. That leaves stealing it, which will also get the cops after me. Unless—

Frank suddenly realized he did have one possible source for the equipment he needed. He didn't dare call ahead. If the man Frank was going to hit up for this stuff got advance warning, he might call the police.

Frank decided to head back out of town. His destination was a low, sprawling building, originally a prosperous farmer's house. But as Frank turned in at the gate he was met with a high-tech security system. A video camera whirred on a swivel mount, and a man's suspicious voice asked who it was in Swedish. At least that's what Frank guessed he asked.

Frank rolled down the window so the camera could see his face. "It's Frank Hardy, Mr. Linska. I need your help."

"Ah," Rutger Linska said. A second later the gate swung open. As Frank drove up to the house he found the small, slender Linska standing by the entrance.

"The police have been here, you know," the engineer said abruptly, but a smile played across his pale face. "I didn't get a chance to thank you. If you hadn't stepped in to help, I would have been arrested as an arms smuggler."

"Well, you can show your thanks in a practical way." Frank went on to explain the situation, ending, "I need some high-tech equipment to keep track of Joe and get to the American end of this people-smuggling gang."

Linska nodded, an amused glint in his eyes. "You came to the right person," he said, leading the way inside. "I've collected a lot of electronic toys."

Frank stared around Rutger Linska's den. It was lined with shelves, and each shelf held some technical marvel.

"Hmmm," the researcher said, surveying his collection. "This would be useful." He took down two boxes, one about the size of a cigarette pack with trailing wires, the other larger

45

with an aerial. "A tracking device. The small box, the transmitter, is good for eight kilometers, approximately five miles. Just let the wires dangle. And don't wind them together."

He ranged over other shelves, coming up with button-size bugging microphones, a larger tracking set, a shotgun mike, a cellular phone. To this pile he added what looked like a fat binder. Actually, it was a notebook computer.

"Super-density hard disk—complete with language-translation programs and a built-in modem for communications. Will all this do?"

Frank shook his head. "It's more than I hoped for," he admitted.

Linska stepped out of the room for a moment, then stepped back in with a soft-sided suitcase. He loaded the equipment inside. Then he tossed something that glittered and jingled over to Frank—car keys.

"You mentioned that you, ah, borrowed the car you're driving," Linska said. "Leave it here. I'll get rid of it. You can take my second car. It's a bit old and banged up and should fit in well in the neighborhood you described."

The scientist smiled. "Just give me a call so I know where you've left it."

"Rutger," Frank said, half in shock. "I can't thank you enough—"

"No, I can't thank *you*," Linska said. "You saved my reputation."

He went back to the entrance to the house

to scan the monitors for the security system. "No one here. I'll take you to the garage."

Linska's second car was a jeeplike vehicle that had seen hard use. This will blend in perfectly, Frank thought as he got behind the wheel, Linska's bag of technological tricks on the seat beside him.

"Thanks again," Frank said.

Linska shook his hand. "Good luck."

The drive back to Stockholm seemed much longer than the trip out. Frank realized how tired he was, and after that realization came the pangs of hunger.

When I get closer to the city, I'll stop off and get something to eat, Frank promised himself.

His stomach rumbles had become a dull roar by the time he reached the outskirts of the city. Frank spotted a small food store on the side of the road and pulled over.

The store owner didn't speak English, but he quickly got the message when Frank pointed at ham, cheese, and bread.

Frank slapped down the first kronor bill he found in his pocket and headed out of the store. He'd reached the door when the shop owner called, *"Hej! Herr!"*

That sounded like, "Hey, mister!"

Frank was just turning back to the man as a gunshot rang out.

Chapter

6

THE BULLET WHIZZED right past Frank's ear to bury itself in the doorpost. Frank snapped out of his tired daze.

He tore back inside the store, tackling the surprised store owner. The man fell backward, bills and coins flying from his hand. My change, Frank realized. That's why he called to me.

He dragged the man down behind the counter, afraid the gunman would now appear in the doorway.

Instead, Frank heard the roar of a car engine and a squeal of tires. By the time he got back to the door, however, his attacker was gone.

The shop owner had finally realized that

48

they'd been shot at, and he remained huddled behind the counter. Frank dashed outside and got into his car. With luck, he'd be out of there without the man getting his license plate number.

Frank had gone half a mile before he realized he'd left his sandwich on the floor.

But then, he had worse things to worry about. Who had shot at him? And why? The why was unpleasantly obvious—the smugglers were after him. "Maybe," Frank whispered, "the shooter is the same sniper who murdered Jumsai Khoo—"

Frank shook his head. The spurt of adrenaline that had sped him up in the food shop must be wearing off, he thought. He was getting tired and thickheaded. Abdul Deharr had shot Khoo and had been captured moments after. More likely, the triggerman was the same person who had firebombed the safe house where he and Joe had hidden out.

That raised the most disturbing question—how had the gunman found him? Frank was sure that he and Joe had successfully disappeared into the crowd. He'd have willingly sworn that no one had followed them.

Obviously, though, someone had. How could Frank be sure that he wasn't being followed now?

If Frank headed back to the smugglers' safe house, he might lead the gunman straight to

Joe—and get them both killed. If he stayed away from the safe house, Joe might disappear, and Frank would lose him forever.

Driving on through the night, Frank finally decided to keep circling the neighborhood where Joe was being kept. At least he'd be close by. He'd also be a moving target.

Joe Hardy sat in an armchair with springs poking up in a corner of the living room. He'd chosen it on purpose because no one standing in the hallway could see him there. Joe snapped awake when he heard one of the guards boisterously shout, "Yah, Klaus, you take it easy, now."

A moment later Joe heard the apartment door slam shut. A weight rolled off his shoulders. Klaus was gone!

One of the guards stepped into the room and pointed at Fuat Dere. "You, come in here."

Looking apprehensive, the young man walked down the hall. He didn't return.

Next the Wongs were called, then Gustav Strular. Finally it was Joe's turn.

The guard pointed to a room off the hallway. Joe stepped in, the door slammed, and a bank of brilliant floodlights came on. Joe froze, blinking.

"Try to look a little less shifty-eyed," a voice commanded from behind the lights.

"What?" Joe began. Then he began to make out the shape of a camera behind the lights.

"Hey, we don't have all night to take your new passport picture."

Joe glanced behind him. A large piece of beige poster paper had been tacked to the door.

"Come on! We don't want your profile."

Joe turned face-forward, trying to appear natural. The camera clicked. "Okay," another voice said. "There's a fresh shirt and jacket on that chair. Put them on."

As Joe changed the photo lights were turned off. The photographer handed a picture to a skinny old man sitting behind a small table. The man glued the photo down, then hammered something against it.

"Done!" the man said, smile wrinkles appearing at the corners of his mouth. He beckoned Joe over, holding out a small dark green booklet. It was a passport, Joe realized, from the Republic of Ireland. Opening it, he saw that it was made out to Ron Grady. But now it had Joe Hardy's picture, embossed with an official seal.

The forger gave him a pen. "Sign here."

Joe wrote "Ron Grady" on the dotted line. "How did you do the seal?" he asked.

"Oh, there are fast-acting plastics that take

51

the impression, then get hard enough to hammer onto the picture," the man said.

"And the passport?"

"Let's just say that Ron Grady won't be needing it anymore. Go back to the parlor. Mr. Ducats wants to speak to you all."

Joe stepped into the living room to find that his fellow travelers had changed, too. Fuat Dere's mustache was carefully trimmed, and he wore trendy, expensive clothing. Strular was dressed in a dull plaid sports jacket and too-short slacks. The Wongs were in brightly colored tourist clothes, with odd, floppy cloth hats. Cheng Wong had a camera around his neck. "I—I never have something worth so much money. What do I do?"

"Take lots of pictures with it. You'll look just like a tourist," Ducats said, a smile crossing his plump features. "You'll all be tourists when you arrive in Copenhagen."

"Copenhagen?" Joe said, then wished he hadn't spoken as four guards glared at him.

"You will be leaving very soon to catch the first flight," Ducats said. "Sven here will be your tour guide."

He paused for a second, giving Joe a hard look. "Obey him as you love your life."

Frank stifled a yawn as he pulled the car up in front of the house. He'd driven all night, taking all sorts of precautions to spot any followers. Nothing—and no one—had shown up. Finally he'd decided it was safe enough to park and check the place out.

Pulling into an alley across the street from the dingy building, he opened his bag of equipment and took out the shotgun mike. Frank aimed the long-range microphone at the window that had lit up when Joe arrived the night before.

No sound came through. The room was empty.

Oh, no, Frank thought. The apartment had emptied out while he circled the area. It must have taken only minutes.

He dashed across the street. He flew up the stairs and in a few minutes had the door to the apartment open. A quick run-through showed Frank that the apartment definitely was empty.

Somewhere in that apartment, though, there had to be a clue. Frank knew his brother. If there was any way to leave a hint as to the next stop on the route, Joe would find it.

Frank almost stepped on the clue. It was a paper airplane, folded in the distinctive way Joe had of making them. The plane even had U.S. written on the wings in Joe's handwriting.

Crumpling the paper plane in his hand, Frank ran out the door and down the stairs.

Stockholm had only one airport. He'd catch up with Joe at Arlanda Airport.

Frank covered the distance to the airport in record time. He parked his somewhat battered jeep in the airport parking lot and picked up the suitcase Rutger Linska had given him.

I'd better remember to give Linska a call, Frank thought as he headed for the main terminal. Prowling the international departures area, he started looking for his brother.

Frank's eye passed over a young man in a green jacket—one more blond guy in a country of blonds. Then his attention was jerked back. It was Joe! He had changed his clothes.

Keeping his brother in sight from the corner of his eye, Frank watched as Joe and several other tourists filed into the waiting area for an international flight. Frank walked on, memorizing the flight data, flight number, airline name, and time of departure, which would be in twenty minutes. He also noted the destination—Copenhagen.

Frank dashed for the ticket counter. Using his credit card, he quickly became the proud owner of a ticket to Copenhagen.

"You'd better hurry," the ticket attendant said. "The flight is leaving from gate—"

"I know," Frank said quickly. He hurried back to the departure gate, his bag in his hand. As he ran he heard a jingle in his pocket—Linska's car keys.

It'll only take a moment to let him know where the car is, Frank told himself. He spotted an old-fashioned telephone booth tucked behind some vending machines and sprinted for it, pushing a heavyset woman aside.

Frank peered through the glass door at the woman frowning at him. "One minute," he promised, raising an index finger.

Frank dialed Linska's office number. He suspected the researcher was the early-to-the-office type. "Linska," a familiar voice said.

"It's Frank Hardy. I'm at Arlanda Airport. Your car is in the long-term—"

Frank turned in annoyance as someone pushed the phone-booth door open. "I said I'd be out in a min—"

It wasn't the woman he'd cut in front of. Frank stared surprised at a man in dark clothes and spiky hair who stood blocking the doorway.

Then he saw the gloved hand with the knife coming straight for his chest.

Frank had nowhere to run.

Chapter

7

THE DARK-CLAD MAN grinned savagely as his knife stabbed at the helpless Frank Hardy. Then the man's expression changed as a heavy hand landed on his shoulder.

"Jeg er næste!" A furious frown showed on the meaty face of the woman Frank had beaten to the phone. Frank didn't need a translator. She was protesting that she was next to use the booth.

Frank also didn't need a cue to use this split-second distraction. He slammed the door on his attacker's wrist. Reflexively the man's hand opened, and the knife clattered to the floor.

The woman never saw the knife—it was hidden by the assassin's body. She was now speaking very loudly in Swedish to him because she must have decided he was cutting in front of her, too.

Attention was the last thing the assassin wanted. He yanked himself free and dashed away.

Frank couldn't afford to find himself in official hands either. "Mr. Linska?" he said into the phone.

"What's going on there?" Rutger Linska asked.

"You wouldn't believe it if I told you." Frank dropped his bag to hide the knife from the woman. "I just wanted to tell you that your car is in the long-term parking area. Thanks again for all your help."

Frank picked up his suitcase, at the same time kicking the blade to the rear of the phone booth. "I'm sorry, ma'am," he said to the woman, who was still yelling.

Continuing down the corridor, Frank checked his watch. He still had time to board the flight to Copenhagen.

From the corner of his eye he caught a flurry of movement. Someone had ducked behind a newsstand. Frank pretended to look in his bag. Actually he was using some highly polished metal equipment as a mirror. The reflection showed a man skulking behind him— the man in black who'd tried to knife him.

Perfect, Frank thought. I've got no time to

fool around. If I'm not on that plane, Joe is gone. But how can I lose this guy in five minutes?

He walked on down the corridor, then noticed an access door left ajar. The sign on the door read *Förbjuden*. The word looked enough like "forbidden" for Frank to take a chance. With luck, the door would lock behind him and leave his shadow out in the cold.

Frank picked up his pace, darting for the door. He yanked it open, stepped through, and slammed it, only to have it bounce open again.

Something's wrong with the lock, he realized. Frank didn't hang around. With luck he could still lose his pursuer. He was behind the scenes of the airport, a maze of ducts and catwalks, bare walls and shadows. Frank went down a metal staircase, hoping the noise of a conveyor belt full of suitcases would cover his movement. He reached the rough concrete floor and ran for an area where a forest of pipes and pillars rose to the ceiling. If he could reach that cover unseen—

A chilling laugh floated down from a catwalk above him. "You cannot make it, I am afraid," a soft, slightly accented voice said in English.

Frank didn't stop. He reached a pillar and ducked behind it. A rolling metal cart was parked behind another pillar.

Maybe I can use this as a diversion, Frank thought. He kicked at the cart, sending it rolling noisily in one direction while he darted in the other, crouching to take advantage of some stacked cases.

He crept noiselessly toward an area with several overhead conveyor belts. They should block the view of his attacker. Just as he reached what he thought was safety, Frank heard that mocking laugh again.

"You *are* good," the voice from above said. "I can see why you cost the boss so much money. And I see why the boss calls me to get rid of you. I think it will be easy, driving to the house where you hide. One bomb, I think, and *pfft!* the problem is gone."

"You knew where we were," Frank said, his voice tight. "But it was secret. The police—"

His unseen stalker laughed again. "The boss, he knows what the blue coats know, what you do. So do I."

Frank caught the barest glitter of something flying at him, and he threw himself to one side. A knife hit on the concrete, then skittered away.

"That's two knives you've lost trying to get me," Frank said. "Why not quit while you're ahead?"

Frank dashed through the shadows, trying to keep something solid above him so the man couldn't follow his path. The overhead conveyor belts separated. Frank took the left-hand fork. He saw a metal service ladder dead ahead that led to a valve on a cross-pipe high above.

"You cannot get away. You will die here," the voice said. Frank did notice that the voice was farther away. The killer didn't know where he was!

Silently Frank came up to the ladder. Slipping the strap of his soft-sided case over his shoulder, he began to climb.

His ascent was nerve-racking. Frank had to watch how he placed his feet, where he put his weight. One rattle of the ladder and the killer would know where he was.

Frank finally reached the valve and just hung from the ladder for a moment, catching his breath. He looked down and suddenly saw a dark shape on the catwalk below. Frank was above the killer now. He saw the glitter of a third blade in the assassin's hand.

The man moved silently along the catwalk. The metal bridge he prowled on was about twenty feet off the ground, but Frank was ten feet higher. The horizontal pipe he was level with crossed over that same catwalk!

Taking a deep breath, Frank reached out for the pipe. At least it wasn't carrying hot water. The metal was cool beneath his fingers as he swung free of the ladder, moving hand over hand toward the man in black.

If I have incredible luck, I'll be able to position myself right over him, Frank thought.

Unfortunately, he didn't have that sort of luck. The man must have detected something when Frank was just yards from him. The killer turned, stared up for a second, then brought up his knife for a throw.

Frank took advantage of that second's hesitation to hurl himself onto the catwalk. He landed with a crash that shook the entire bridgework.

The assassin's knife missed.

Frank had landed awkwardly, teetering on the edge of the catwalk. He barely had time to claw himself into a kneeling position before the man was on him.

The killer's plan was obvious—he would hurl Frank to the concrete floor below.

Frank had no time for anything fancy. He unslung the bag from his shoulder and swung the heavy satchel with all his might.

He knew the expression "cut off at the knees," but now Frank Hardy witnessed it. The man's legs buckled, and he clutched at the safety rail. It wasn't enough—he plunged over it with a yell.

The killer's fate was kinder than the one he'd planned for Frank. He flopped facedown onto a conveyor belt and was whisked off to disappear into a black duct.

Frank clattered along the catwalk. If he found the door he'd come through and ran like a maniac, he calculated, he might still make the Copenhagen plane.

The passengers were just boarding when he reached the gate. Frank turned in his ticket, then went to the rear of the line. Spotting another pay telephone, Frank rushed over, joined the line, and pulled out his computer and an acoustical modem hookup. Luckily, the little machine was strongly built. It worked perfectly as Frank accessed the airline's reservation records, erasing all record of his itinerary. Instead he placed himself on the next flight to Trondheim, Norway.

Let the man in black follow me there, he said to himself.

Frank was the last aboard the plane. He'd splurged on a first-class ticket, so he was at the front of the plane. He did get a glance into the coach section as he went to his seat, however. Joe Hardy was sitting in the third row back.

Sinking into his seat, Frank closed his eyes for the first time in almost twenty-four hours and was asleep before the plane took off.

Rank has its privileges. For instance, first-class passengers on airplanes always exit be-

fore the travelers in coach. So Frank Hardy
was off the plane and ready to follow his
brother well before Joe reached the arrival
gate.

Sven, the guard in charge of the group, had
told his human cargo they were to arrive sepa-
rately at the Norden Hotel.

Joe took a taxi to downtown Copenhagen,
not taking in the storybook charm of the mel-
low brick buildings with red or tarnished green
roofs. Was he being followed? And if so, by
whom?

Shortly afterward Joe arrived at the Norden
Hotel, a modest five-story brick building with
cast-iron balconies. At least it doesn't look
like a dump, Joe thought as he took the small
carry-on bag provided by the smugglers and
walked in to register as Ron Grady.

"Ah, yes, Mr. Grady," the desk clerk said
in perfect English, "you're part of the Wanderfree tour group."

Joe wondered who had invented that sick
name for the smuggling operation.

"You'll be in room four hundred eight," the
clerk went on, handing over a key.

Moments later Joe stepped into his room
and dropped into a chair. After a few minutes
he rose and unpacked his bag. Joe was already
pulling off his shirt, anticipating a long
shower, when an abrupt knock sounded on his
door.

"Who is it?" Joe asked.

"Sven," a flat voice answered from outside. "Open up."

Joe opened the door, and Sven stepped in. "We eat in the restaurant tonight. Nobody leaves the hotel," he said, his voice menacing. "Be ready to leave by nine o'clock tomorrow morning. We want to beat the crowds at Tivoli Gardens."

"Tivoli?" Joe blinked. "Isn't that an amusement park or something?"

"Right," Sven said. "It will be very amusing."

Outside room 408, Frank Hardy removed the bug from the door. Tivoli Gardens, nine A.M. He'd be ready.

After his shower Joe napped. It was evening by the time he emerged from his room refreshed, rested, and starving. He took the elevator down and searched the lobby for a place to eat. The hotel restaurant was pleasant, paneled in light wood with a cream-colored ceiling. A big buffet table loaded with food dominated the center of the room. The walls were lined with triple rows of small tables with comfortable-looking chairs.

The table closest to the door was taken by Gustav Strular and one of the guards. They had their heads together, talking in low tones. Joe stared. What do a prisoner and his guard have to chat about?

Strular's watery blue eyes narrowed in—what? suspicion? annoyance?—when Joe walked in.

Joe returned the gaze, keeping up the staring contest even as he walked into the restaurant, and bumped into someone.

"Oh, sorry," Joe said, stepping back. From the impact he knew the person he'd run into was soft, warm, and feminine. Now he saw that she was young, tall, with a slim, athletic figure and shoulder-length black hair.

"I hope I didn't hurt you," Joe said as the young woman turned around.

The smile froze on his face. That golden skin, the high cheekbones, the jade green eyes—he knew this girl.

Joe's heart beat faster, but not from romance. As pretty as she was, he'd been chasing her for another reason. She was one of the people to escape the downfall of Phoenix's Stockholm operation.

The girl was Ilsa Marie Khoo.

Chapter

8

ILSA KHOO'S EYES grew wide when she saw Joe. "What—" she began, stopping as she stared over Joe's shoulder.

Joe turned to see Mr. Ducats standing behind them. "It's all right, my little cargoes. It's all in the family, you might say. Sit together," the plump man said. "Just stop drawing attention to yourselves and let the other guests get to the food."

"This gentleman is with us?" Ilsa asked, looking at Joe. Still, Joe noticed, she didn't say a word to denounce him.

"Yes, Mr. Grady is part of our wonderful Wanderfree tour," Ducats said. "There's no reason in the world why you shouldn't sit with him, Ms. Tamani. Who knows? Maybe you'll even enjoy a shipboard romance."

"We'll see," Ilsa said cryptically as the plump man led them out of the flow of patrons beginning to enter the restaurant.

"So, would you like to eat together?" Joe asked.

Ilsa gave him an ironic smile. "I couldn't think of anything more interesting, Mr.—what was that name again? Grady?"

Joe glanced around. Ducats had moved to the buffet table. Strular was still giving him the evil eye. "That's right. Ron Grady. And what's your first name, Ms. *Tamani?*" He put a little emphasis on Ilsa's smuggling alias.

"It's Imako," she said. "A fine old Japanese name. Imako Tamani."

"Very nice," Joe responded. "It sounds almost made for you."

Ilsa ignored the dig. "Shall we try the food?"

They stepped over to the buffet table, which was covered with delicacies Joe couldn't identify. "So this is a smorgasbord," Joe said, impressed.

A young woman filling her plate gave him a hard look. "Maybe they call it that in Sweden," she said. "But here in Denmark we call it the *koldt bord.*"

"Sorry," Joe muttered. He handed Ilsa a plate, took one for himself, and gingerly poked a server into a bowl full of long brownish objects.

67

"I wouldn't have thought you'd like smoked eel," Ilsa said sweetly.

Joe hurriedly pulled his hand back. "How about these?" he asked, gesturing at the next row of bowls.

"Herring," Ilsa told him. "Smoked, pickled, and in cream sauce."

"Don't they eat anything but fish around here?" Joe muttered.

"In the old days that was the only source of protein they could depend on," Ilsa said.

"Now here's something I recognize," Joe said. "Smoked salmon."

Ilsa nodded. "That's gravlax. It goes with the mustard sauce. They used to store it by burying it underground. That's how it got its name. The *grav* in gravlax comes from the same word as *grave* in English." She gave Joe an evil grin. "The name means 'salmon from the grave.'"

Joe stared at her. "You really know how to help a guy enjoy a meal."

Still, he took some of the salmon and several thick slices of black bread, then went down the table to discover other delicacies. In the end his plate was loaded with two kinds of ham, a spicy chicken salad, tiny meatballs, fresh potato salad, and a salad of cucumbers and onions in vinegar.

"You don't have to take everything at

once," Ilsa cautioned. "They let you come back as often as you like."

They found a table far from the other Wanderfree travelers and sat down to eat. Joe found himself remembering the good times they'd had in Stockholm, but he couldn't let himself forget that the last time he'd seen Ilsa her father had led him off to kill him. Maybe she'd been involved, too.

"So, Ms. Tamani," he said, keeping up the pretense of just meeting her, "are you traveling alone?"

Ilsa stared down at her plate. "I was with an important businessman," she said, circling around the facts. "But he went on ahead—first class." Her lips quirked.

"And where is 'on ahead'?" Joe asked.

"I know only as much as you do," Ilsa admitted. "We're to be ready to go to Tivoli in the morning."

"I wish I understood that," Joe said. "What's the idea of taking us to an amusement park?"

"It's more than that," Ilsa said excitedly. "There are rides, of course. But there are also gardens, restaurants, concerts and shows, a marching band. . . ." She smiled. "When I was a little girl I thought Tivoli was the most wonderful place on earth. My father would take me there—"

She broke off, and the light went out of her

eyes. That was all in the past now, Joe realized. Those were the happy days before Jumsai Khoo had become a fugitive from the law, before his partners had had him killed.

They sat in silence for a moment, Ilsa focusing on her food, trying not to cry. Joe watched as a familiar figure behind her crossed the dining room. It was Frank.

"I think I'll leave you for a moment," Joe said to her. As he rose from the table he saw Frank step through a door marked *Herrer* and decorated with the outline of a man.

A moment later Joe stepped into the men's room, too. A quick glimpse around showed that the place was empty except for his brother.

"Even undercover you pick up the girls," Frank said. "I could only see her from the rear where I was sitting. Is she pretty?"

"She's Ilsa Khoo," Joe said.

Frank's eyebrows rose. "Is Bremer here?"

"She says he's gone on ahead. Probably on business."

Frank gave his brother a concerned look. "She told you that much? I don't know if that's a good sign. Maybe she's setting you up—"

"She could have already blown my cover here," Joe said, "but she didn't." He frowned, adding, "But it might be better if she didn't know you were around."

"I'll keep a low profile," Frank promised. "So, have you heard anything more about your itinerary, besides the trip to the Tivoli Gardens?"

Joe stared. "How did you know about that?"

"A little bug told me." Frank explained about the equipment he'd gotten from Rutger Linska. He also reported his two run-ins with the assassin.

"Great," Joe said, "as if we didn't have enough problems. You be careful, Frank."

"Funny," Frank said, "I was about to tell you the same thing."

Joe went to the door. "I'll give it a rap if it's safe to come out—you know, if Ilsa isn't looking this way."

He stepped out and scanned the room. Ilsa wasn't sitting at their table anymore. She had joined the Wongs and was leaning over their table. Joe knocked on the door, then walked over to Ilsa, coming in on the middle of a conversation.

"We were at university together," Cheng Wong was saying. "We graduated into a country where we didn't fit in, where the government was suspicious of us. We married, but they wanted to put us on farms hundreds of miles apart. So we run away."

So that's what they're hiding from, Joe thought.

Lu Wong whispered in her husband's ear. He nodded. "My wife says no more talk of what we were yesterday. We do what we have to do now." He looked down in embarrassment at the camera that still hung on his chest. "And we hope for a better tomorrow."

Together the couple got up from their table and left the restaurant, holding hands.

Ilsa's face was solemn as she watched them go. Then she turned to Joe. "Mr. Ducats signed for all our dinners, so we're all paid up." She glanced at the buffet table. "Unless you want more."

Joe decided to try to lighten the mood. "What? And have you tell me more bizarre things about the food I'm eating?"

That got a grin from Ilsa. "They said we can't leave the hotel. But there's a disco downstairs."

"And the night is still young," Joe said. Together they left the restaurant.

The disco was a long, narrow room in the cellar of the hotel. Brick walls bounced back blaring dance music. But the music was good, Ilsa's dancing was excellent, and for a little while Joe managed to forget all about the case.

However, the real world soon intruded in the form of Sven, their burly guard.

The big man cut in on them.

Joe made sure he got the next dance—a

slow one—and whispered in Ilsa's ear, "From now on we'll have to put up with that big ape."

"No," she said back, "I've had enough dancing tonight."

Ilsa's room was on the top floor of the hotel. She and Joe rode up in the elevator, and Joe saw her to her door, room 521.

"It was a good night tonight," Ilsa said.

"Best I've had in a while," Joe admitted.

"For me, too." Ilsa raised her face, and her soft lips brushed Joe's. "Thanks, Joe Hardy," she whispered.

Joe stood outside the door for several moments after Ilsa went in, trying to sort out his feelings. It had been a very good night. He hadn't had fun in a long time.

But was Ilsa the right person to have fun with? Her father had been one of the top smugglers in the Phoenix organization. And she was on the run from the law with the last remaining leader from Phoenix's Stockholm operation. What was her connection with the organization?

Joe couldn't accept Ilsa as a cold-blooded killer, but he'd been wrong about pretty girls in the past.

He heard the stir of footsteps on the carpeted floor and turned to find Fuat Dere walking down the hall toward him.

"We cannot go out on the street," the Turk

73

said, "but there are balconies, at least." He pointed down the hall, which ended in French doors opening onto a small terrace surrounded by a waist-high iron railing.

"It even looks out over a garden," Dere said, heading to his own room.

Maybe that's what I need, Joe thought, a little fresh air. He walked down the hall and through the open doors. The iron rail around the balcony was twisted in intricate and lacy shapes. Joe leaned against it, staring at the hotel's garden, five stories down.

Couples wandered below hand in hand. Joe thought of Ilsa again.

Then he turned his mind away from that distraction. Was this the usual route for the people smugglers? he wondered. Had his father perhaps stood on a balcony like this, taking in this view? Where was Fenton Hardy now? Was he all right?

Joe was so deep in his thoughts that he missed the faint movement behind him. His first hint that he wasn't alone on the balcony came when a pair of heavy hands landed on his back. By then it was too late.

Joe had been pushed over the railing and was falling toward the pretty garden below.

Chapter

9

JOE KICKED and twisted wildly in midair, clawing for any sort of hold. He managed to grasp one of the ornate iron swirls that made up the balcony railing.

Joe held on for only a moment before his hand slipped free. But the action slowed his fall long enough for his other hand to catch onto the terrace of the balcony itself. Joe was pulling himself up when a heavy shoe stomped down on his exposed fingers. His grip weakened, and he felt himself slipping.

If I'm going down, I'd better make sure I don't go far, Joe thought. He swung his legs in toward the building as he lost his grip.

Joe dropped to the railing of the balcony on the floor below, teetering between the safety of the platform and a further fall of three stories. His arms windmilled desperately as he fought for balance. With one final burst Joe threw himself onto the terrace.

He collapsed there, his back to the metal rail. His breath came in ragged gasps. As soon as he could, Joe staggered to his feet and went up the stairs to the fifth floor.

Not surprisingly, the hallway was empty. Joe went to Ilsa's room and knocked on the door. Maybe she had heard someone out here, he thought.

Or maybe you just want her to kiss it and make it better, another part of Joe's mind jeered.

In the end, it didn't matter. Ilsa didn't answer the door. Joe knocked again, stopping when he realized he was pounding on the door. Wherever Ilsa was, she certainly wasn't in her room.

Joe went downstairs to his own quarters. He soaked his bruised hand in a basin full of cold water.

When he felt somewhat human again Joe headed down to the lobby. I'll just take a stroll through the lobby to see if I can spot anyone, Joe told himself.

The restaurant was empty now, but the lobby lounge held a scattering of people. Seated in a deep armchair, speaking intently with one of the enforcers, was Gustav Strular.

The small, pale man was speaking very emphatically when he spotted Joe. Immediately he pulled back, muttering something to his companion.

The guard turned to give Joe a long, hard stare. Joe recognized him by the scar on his face. This was the guy who'd been at the door of the smugglers' Stockholm safe house.

For a second Joe considered stepping up and challenging them about his little plunge off the balcony upstairs. Then he thought better of it. He wouldn't find out anything, even if Strular was responsible. The German was so buddy-buddy with the scar-faced enforcer, they'd probably alibi each other and give Joey Tate a reputation as a troublemaker.

Well, maybe I'm in the mood to make a little trouble, Joe thought. He picked up a piece of hotel notepaper and folded it. "Can I leave a note for Herr Strular?" he said, going up to the reception desk.

"Strular, yes," the clerk said, taking the paper, then turning to a set of pigeonholes behind the desk. She put the note in a box marked 517.

"Thanks a lot," Joe said, heading for the elevator. He pressed the button for the fifth floor. Now I know Strular's room is 517, and while he's still in the lounge I'll pay it a little visit.

The smugglers had checked Joe for ID,

money, and weapons. They hadn't paid much attention to the little laminated calendar Joe carried in his pocket. That was all he needed to get past the old-fashioned door lock on room 517.

He gave the closet a quick once-over, finding nothing very interesting. Strular had been outfitted by the smugglers as a nerdy guy with no taste. Joe also noticed some well-tailored suits made with expensive fabric, clothes that Strular must have owned. Oddly, these all had the makers' labels removed.

The bathroom provided no hiding places. All Joe found were the usual toiletries and a hairbrush with several mousy brown hairs caught in the bristles. He was about to turn away when he noticed something odd about the can of shaving cream lying next to the brush on the bathroom sink. The bright green cap was on, and there seemed to be an extra collar of metal between the cap and the painted body of the can.

Joe picked up the cream container—and something rattled in the bottom of the can. After a moment's inspection he twisted the metal top, and the container came apart in two sections. In Joe's right hand was what appeared to be another can of shaving cream. In his left was a metal cylinder just large enough to cover the real can of cream.

Joe had read about setups like this. They

were used to smuggle film, photos, or thin paper. But something was rattling in the bottom of the cylinder.

Putting down the can of cream, Joe emptied the cylinder into his right palm. Out rolled a small scrap of material, red, black, and gold, with a pin attached on one end and a medal on the other.

Joe stared. A military medal? He couldn't translate the motto stamped into the metal, but he did recognize the three letters, SSD. Joe had lived through some brushes with the world of espionage, had studied up on the various spy and security organizations of the world. Those three letters represented the Staatssicherheitsdienst, or State Security Service, secret police of the old East Germany.

With the end of the East German government, a lot of people who'd wielded power under the dictatorship had had to flee. If Gustav Strular was a member of the dreaded Stasi, as the secret police was commonly known, he'd probably have a lot to answer for.

Joe shook his head. Strular's vanity had been his downfall. Unable to part with his precious medal, he had concealed it in a hiding place that wasn't exactly right for the job.

Well, I learned *something* from this little jaunt, Joe thought as he returned the medal to its hiding place. Then he headed out the door.

Joe had barely gotten three steps down the hallway when an agitated Gustav Strular came charging along. The German had a crumpled piece of notepaper in his hand.

"What are you doing here?" Strular demanded. "You do not belong on this floor."

"What's your problem?" Joe asked.

"I get my key, and the desk clerk says there is a message for me. But the message is just a blank piece of paper. I rush up here and find you near my room. Perhaps you were inside it."

"Hey, I was just walking down the hall," Joe said, going into his Joey Tate impersonation. "I don't know why you're so bent out of shape. It's a free country, isn't it?"

Strular pushed past, muttering.

Joe decided to take the stairs down. He was just about to descend when he heard the elevator door opening on the fifth floor.

"It's been a long day," a voice said.

Joe froze. That was Ilsa Khoo!

"And a fun night." Joe recognized that voice, too. It belonged to Sven.

Noiselessly Joe stepped back so he had a view of the whole hallway. Ilsa and Sven were in front of her room. He had her in a bear hug, lifting her right off the floor. "Yeah, fun," Sven said.

"But now the fun is over," Ilsa said, untangling herself.

"Sure you don't want some company?" Sven asked as she opened her door.

"Positive," she said. "You wouldn't want to make us late getting to Tivoli, would you?"

Joe let go of a deep breath he was holding when the big man shrugged and walked away. I think I've had enough for one night, Joe thought, heading down the stairs. The sooner I get to sleep, the better.

When he went down for breakfast the next morning, Joe found Mr. Ducats waiting for him in the lobby. The plump man wore a jacket and cap with the words Wanderfree Tours on them. "Come and join the group, Mr. Grady," he said.

The Wongs were already present, as were Fuat Dere, Strular, and Ilsa. In addition there was an older man wearing sunglasses, and a moment later a pimply-faced young man with shifty eyes joined them.

"Ah, that makes our full dozen," Ducats said.

Joe had already noticed Sven, the scarfaced man, and two other burly enforcers wearing resort wear.

Ducats ushered them into the restaurant, where Joe noticed Frank Hardy seated by himself at a table. Frank had left by the time the phony tour director led the others out to a waiting minibus.

The entrance to Tivoli was a big arch in pinkish stone topped by a greenish copper dome. Ducats paid for tickets, and in they all went.

Joe was surprised at his first look at the place. It looked awfully green for an amusement park. The main road in front of them was lined with trees. "I guess they really mean it when they call this place a garden," he said to Ilsa.

"I suppose," she said, moving away.

Joe's lips tightened. She had sat beside Sven on the way over, and now this. It was as if she didn't want to be seen with him, or—

Joe suddenly stopped, a less pleasant thought coming to mind. Maybe Ilsa was disappointed to see him. What if she'd set up his little high dive last night?

Sven suddenly appeared beside him, wrapping a brawny arm around Joe's shoulders. "Come on, Ron. We don't want you falling behind now."

For the next couple of hours they acted just like tourists, taking in the rides and attractions. They watched as a brass band came marching by and rode on a wild carousel that rose into the air on a hydraulic pump. As he whizzed around fifty feet above the ground Joe spotted Frank below, shadowing the group.

They also rode on an ancient roller coaster.

The slopes weren't so bad, but Joe's nerves were on edge for the entire ride, thanks to the loud creaking from the wooden track and supports. It sounds as if it's going to collapse, he thought.

Joe noticed that Sven must have felt the same way. His knuckles were white as he gripped the safety bar.

It was after the roller-coaster ride that the big blond man went over to Ducats. Joe was just lucky to overhear as Sven murmured, "Somebody is following us. A dark-haired teenager. He's been on or hanging around every ride we've gone to."

"We'll take care of him." Ducats reached out to grab Sven's arm as the big man started to move away. "But not here. Wait till we're in the dark."

They split up, and Joe frowned. In the dark? What did that mean?

A few moments later Joe understood the meaning as they were herded into a haunted house. The spooky route was full of shadows, dark enough for "taking care" of anyone.

Joe hung back from the group, hoping to warn Frank. Instead, retracing his steps in the darkness, he bumped into Sven. The big man was standing by the medieval torture dungeon display. He'd removed the executioner dummy and just slipped on the leather vest the figure had worn. Sven had the executioner's mask in one hand and a big, heavy ax in the other.

"What are you doing here?" Sven demanded.

"I dropped my—"

"Forget it," the big man said. "Get back with the group. That's an order."

Joe still hesitated. "What are *you* doing?" he asked.

Sven put on the hood. "Preparing a little surprise." He ran a finger down the edge of the ax. "Surprisingly sharp."

Muscles tensed in Joe's arms. He had to stop this!

Then another heavy hand landed on his shoulder. It was another guard, the one with the scarred face. "Come on," he said. "They've opened the panel." He dragged Joe along to join the group.

Joe looked back hopelessly. Sven adopted the dummy's pose, ax upraised.

Any moment now Frank would be along— to get the last shock of his life!

Chapter

10

JOE HARDY STRUGGLED futilely in the grip of
the scar-faced guard. He was hustled along
the gloomy halls of the haunted house past
other scary scenes.

Then Joe and his captor came to a patch
of unexpected brightness. Mr. Ducats held a
flashlight as two guards worked with screw-
drivers to remove a panel from the wall.

"Ah, my young friend," Ducats said with
an edge to his voice. "I was afraid we'd lost
you."

"I dropped something back there," Joe
said. "My good-luck piece."

"Yes? Well, your first piece of bad luck
might have been to get yourself killed," Ducats told him. "Cargo doesn't have personal

85

property. It just goes where it's told—quietly.''

Ahead of them the guards had gotten the panel open and were guiding their human cargo through. Scar-face glanced off down the corridor. "Do we leave the panel open for Sven?" he asked.

"We'll put it back in, but loosely," Ducats decided. "No sense in calling attention to our secret exit."

At the end of the line of illegal travelers Joe was desperately trying to figure some way to mark the spot. His shoulders rubbed against the rough plywood wall, and he got an idea. Reaching into his back pocket, he took out his handkerchief. Ducats was in front of him, and behind, Scar-face was picking up the panel.

Joe rubbed the cotton handkerchief against the plywood until its fibers caught on some splinters. Then he turned to Scar-face. "Need some help with that thing?" he asked, using his body to mask his improvised flag.

The guard grunted and pushed Joe out of his way, more interested in the person blocking his way than the wall beyond. Using a pair of handles on the inside of the panel, Scar-face pulled the barrier in flush with the wall. Four long bolts fit neatly in as many holes, which were drilled in the wooden frame. The man quickly threaded a pair of nuts onto the top two bolts.

Sure, Joe thought. That holds the panel in place, but it can quickly be removed.

The guard turned to Joe. "What are you hanging around for?" he demanded. A moment later Joe was being thrust along through a maze of maintenance tunnels. Then they came to a set of stairs that headed down.

Joe could see the wan glow of a flashlight and the main body of his group. He also heard running water. "What—" he began.

Scar-face pushed him onward. "It's the sewers. Don't worry, you won't have to go swimming. There's a raised path. And then we're in the clear."

Too bad the guard never mentioned the sewer stink, Joe thought, holding his hand over his nose as he shuffled along the slimy stone walkway. He watched as the party slipped one by one through a huge crack in the wall. When he went through he found himself in another tunnel, with train tracks nearby.

"We are now under the central railway station," Ducats told the group. "You will follow me up to the platforms, then up to street level, where we will find transportation to the next stage of our journey."

Joe's shoulders sagged. Even if Frank gets past that goon with the ax, he thought, how will he catch up with us?

*   *   *

I hope I didn't let them get too far ahead, Frank Hardy thought, picking up his pace as he moved through the haunted house. He pressed on through the darkness, hardly paying attention to the horrors that were supposed to scare him.

At least I can use the shadows for cover and get close again, Frank thought. The darkness was replaced by dim light as he came to another horror tableau—a dungeon scene with an executioner dummy holding a raised ax.

Frank was almost at the masked figure when a shuddering rumble sounded overhead.

Right, Frank thought, glancing up. Some sort of roller coaster that passes on the roof.

Then he realized that the dummy had also looked up.

It was a split second of warning, but that was all Frank needed. He launched himself forward in a karate kick as the executioner swung his ax down. Frank's arm slashed upward, knocking the unwieldy weapon aside.

The heavy blade fell harmlessly down. At the same time Frank's extended foot connected with the stomach of the disguised attacker. The man folded in the middle with a great whoosh of lost breath. He tried to grab Frank, but Frank had already slipped past him.

Frank grabbed the ends of the man's mask, twisting it so the eyeholes were shifted away.

The man stumbled blindly, smashing into dungeon props, clawing with one hand to restore his vision while swinging his other arm violently in great sweeps.

But Frank was behind the man, picking up a piece of torture equipment—an iron bar glowing red at one end. Actually, Frank realized, it was just a stout length of wood painted to simulate a red-hot iron. As he hefted it, though, Frank thought it would serve his need perfectly.

His attacker had finally torn the confining mask off, but not before he'd stumbled across the outflung limbs of a group of dummy corpses piled at the rear of the display. The man was on his hands and knees, trying to get up as Frank stepped behind him and swung the stick with all his might.

With a groan the blond man collapsed onto the pile, unconscious.

Good, Frank thought. He looks natural there. He stepped back, clattering into some shackles and chains hanging from a wall. Frank grinned as he discovered some of the hardware was real. In a moment he had cuffed his attacker's hands and feet, then gagged him.

Frank looked around at the mess they'd made. I suppose we should pay for all this, he thought.

Then he noticed a fat wallet on the floor. It

had apparently popped out from his attacker's pocket. Frank scooped it up to find it full of hundred-dollar bills.

Sure, American dollars—the currency of international illegality, he thought. He left a couple of hundreds pinned to the unconscious man's vest as a payment, then pocketed the rest of the money. Might as well let the smugglers' dirty cash help do them in, Frank thought. Besides, I'm running pretty low.

As Frank was about to return the wallet a slip of paper fluttered out. " 'Copenhagen yacht harbor—berth 215b,' " Frank read aloud, holding it up to the dim light. "Well, I've got someplace to try if I lose track of Joe now." He set off down the corridor.

Frank found Joe's handkerchief and popped open the sealed panel, but he had lost all trace of the smugglers by the time he reached the train station. Stepping outside, he hailed a cab. "To the yacht harbor, please," he said.

He arrived at berth 215b to watch a tubby fishing boat pulling out. Among the people on deck was Joe Hardy. Frank stared as the boat cruised off.

What do I do now? Frank's numb thoughts were interrupted by an argument from the next dock.

"Come on, Evie," a young Danish man was saying to his pretty young companion. "You said you loved my boat."

"That was before I realized you love your boat more than me," the young woman said in a flat American accent. "Well, I hope you enjoy it—all by yourself!" She stormed off along the dock.

"Crazy Americans!" the young man swore, kicking a cooler full of food and drink into the water. "I get the day off, and now she leaves me with nothing."

"Excuse me," Frank said, walking over to the young man. "I couldn't help overhearing what just happened."

The young man gave him a wary look. "And?"

Frank grinned. "I just happen to be a crazy American, too. I need a boat to follow that ship out there." He pointed to the departing vessel. "And I think you're just the man to help me." Frank pulled four hundred-dollar bills from his pocket.

"Well, Mr. Crazy *Rich* American, you've just hired yourself a boat. Hop aboard!" Frank and the young man boarded. In moments they had cast off.

Out at sea Joe Hardy was still trying to recover from the sudden change of events. A bus had been waiting for them at the train station. When they got on they discovered their bags were already aboard. "We're leaving the country," Ducats had announced. "If any of you suffer from seasickness, we have pills. . . ."

They had boarded the boat and immediately gone below to change into new clothes and receive new passports and identities.

Now dressed in hiking clothes, Joe stood on deck. He was all on his own. Frank could never catch up. Joe only hoped he hadn't been killed. Joe would be all the help Fenton Hardy could hope for.

A jeering voice sounded in his ear. "Well, the young *Amerikaner* doesn't look so tough now, eh?" Gustav Strular said. "Maybe a little seasick?"

"The only thing to make people sick around here is you, Strudel," Joe snapped back. He turned to the other travelers. "Anybody know where we're going?"

"One of the crew mentioned something about the island of Rügen."

"Ach, Rügen," Strular said nostalgically. "I had a holiday cottage there once."

"Those must have been the good old days, Strudel," Joe said, "back when you were riding high as a Stasi spy. I wonder if you're really so glad to be heading back to Germany."

Strular whipped around to confront Joe, his fists clenched.

"Make your move, Strudel," Joe said.

One of the guards quickly shouldered between the two. "No fighting," he said roughly, "unless you want to swim the rest of the way. The boss has trouble enough. Sven didn't catch up to us before we sailed."

They moved to opposite ends of the boat, Joe suddenly hopeful that Frank might have overwhelmed Sven and might be all right.

"Was that wise, Joe?" Ilsa asked, joining him at the bow.

"Maybe not," he admitted. "But there's something about that guy that makes me want to crush him like a bug."

"Båden!" one of the ship's crew suddenly cried.

"Another boat," Ilsa translated.

Ducats called everyone together. "Get ready for transfer," he said.

"Transfer?" Joe repeated.

"You leave on a Danish boat and arrive on a German one," the head smuggler explained. "We use cables and a canvas chair. It is no trouble."

The German boat was soon alongside, a low-slung fishing trawler. German sailors threw a line to the Danes while Ducats's enforcers brought out the canvas chair. It was more like an open-topped sack with leg holes. Several support lines ran up to a D-ring, which clipped the whole rig onto a pulley.

"You put your legs through, hold on tight, and we pull. Who goes first?"

Fuat Dere, a little gray-faced as he looked at the cable stretched between the two bobbing boats, said, "I will."

He stepped into the canvas sack, the sailors threw a line over to the Germans, and in moments he was rolling along the cable to the other ship.

While they hauled the empty seat back Ducats said, "Who next?"

"Why not the *Amerikaner?*" Strular said.

Joe shrugged. "Why not?" He slipped his legs through the openings in the white canvas.

'Makes you look like you're wearing a giant diaper." Ilsa giggled.

The scar-faced guard checked the rigging, then nodded.

German sailors began hauling, and Joe was swept out between the ships.

Halfway across Joe heard a sharp click overhead.

He looked up and saw that the clip on the ring holding him to the pulley had broken off! Instead of a D-ring it was a C-ring, one side completely open. One good jolt would dislodge him.

Then somebody pulled too hard on the towline, the pulley jostled—

And Joe Hardy dropped straight down— deep into the cold waters of the Baltic Sea.

Chapter

11

JOE GASPED IN SHOCK at his sudden impact with the water. He coughed, choking on a mouthful of salty water as he sank. Still worse was the numbing chill that invaded Joe's body.

He flailed desperately in the entangling folds of canvas and rope. The sodden weight of the transfer apparatus was dragging him down. And as far as Joe could tell, nobody on the surface was doing much to pull him up.

Joe's chest ached from the stress of holding his breath when he finally got free of the rig. He struck off, swimming desperately for the gleam of light above.

His head broke the surface, and his world went from the deathly silence of the watery world to pandemonium. People were yelling orders and suggestions in several different languages. Joe didn't pay attention. His main interest was in taking in air and keeping his chilled arms and legs treading water.

"Over there!" Fuat Dere's voice cut across the shouting. Then came a splash. Dully, Joe realized that someone had thrown him a life preserver. His arms felt as if they belonged to somebody else as he grabbed hold. He did maintain his grip as he was reeled in, then pulled over the low railing of the trawler.

Joe staggered to his feet and stared across to the Danish vessel and to the disappointed face of Gustav Strular.

Looks like he's had two cracks at me now, Joe thought. He probably pushed me off that balcony, and the guard who set me up on that canvas contraption is Strular's friend. I'll have to make sure Strular doesn't get a third chance.

German crew members covered Joe in an old blanket and then lent him some clothes. The transfer was delayed while efforts were made to retrieve the canvas seat, but it had sunk without a trace. The rest of the passengers had to travel the way their luggage did— swinging across the water in a fishing net.

Ilsa was the first over. She scrambled out of the net and ran up to Joe, grabbing his hand. "Are you all right?" she asked.

Joe managed a smile and a nod, but his heart wasn't in it. Ilsa seemed genuinely concerned, but Joe didn't know what to make of her—one minute friendly, the next cold to him. She hadn't even gone to the side of the boat when he got dunked. But if she wanted him dead, all she needed to do was whisper a few words in Ducats's ear. What was she up to?

As a protesting Gustav Strular was hoisted over, Joe turned away to scan the sea. Off in the distance he caught a little flash of white. Straining his eyes, he made out the shape of a small motorboat. Even as he watched, it moved on.

What were you expecting? Joe asked himself sarcastically. Your brother Frank and the U.S. Navy?

As soon as everyone was transferred, the two ships reversed course, heading back to their respective countries. Soon Joe saw a shoreline of chalk white cliffs rising ahead of them. This must be the island of Rügen, he thought.

The ship swung around, following the contours of an impressive coastline until it finally came to an inlet that sheltered a small town.

As soon as the vessel tied up at the dock the passengers were led onto land and up to a battered old bus. Joe stared at the sign on the side of the bus in puzzlement. *"Tour-istfahrt,"* he read. "What is this?"

"It means 'tourist travel' in German," Stru-lar answered.

Moments later Joe was sitting in a slightly sprung seat, leaning against a cracked fake-leather headrest that had been repaired with tape. Better get some rest while I can, he told himself. All I have to rely on now is myself.

At that very moment Frank Hardy was dash-ing up from the same dock after having his passport checked, leaving the boat owner to moor his powerboat. "We traveled a good hun-dred and ninety kilometers," the young sailor called after him. "I'll have to refuel for the trip back."

Frank was only interested in the hundred feet or so he needed to cover to reach the parked bus. The last passenger boarded while Frank was scant yards from the back of the bus. Expelling a blast of smoky exhaust, the vehicle began to pull out.

With a final sprint Frank caught up with the bus, yanked something out of his bag, and thrust a hand behind its rear bumper. He slowed, and the bus drove off.

When Frank returned from the bus, his sailor friend was talking with a gray-haired man. Frank went over and tried out some of his German. *"Wo geht der Bus?"* he asked, trying to find out where the bus might be going.

The older man shrugged. "Straslund," he said. "Berlin." Frank's mind was on another problem. The radio tracker he'd attached to the bumper was good for only five miles. Unless he bought or rented a car, and soon, he'd lose track of Joe.

When Frank asked if any cars were available, the man said, *"Autos? Nein."* He shook his head.

With the young sailor's help Frank pressed the issue. Still the man shook his head. *"Mein Trabant ist kaputt,"* he said.

"He has a car manufactured in East Germany," the young Dane said. "A Trabant. Most of them run poorly. His is broken."

"I heard," Frank said. *"Kaputt."*

"Kaputt, ja." Then the man snapped his fingers. *"Das Kraftrad!"* he exclaimed.

Frank stared. "The what?"

"Kraftrad!" The older German fumbled for words for a moment. *"Motorrad!"*

Seeing Frank's puzzled look, the man raised his hands to imaginary handlebars, twisting his wrists to simulate throttles. *"Vroom, vroom!"* he said.

Light dawned. "A motorcycle!" Frank said.

"Ja," responded the man. He tapped his palm. "Dollars."

Frank rolled his eyes. "I'll bet that's the only English this guy speaks."

After parting with most of the American money he had left, Frank got to see the motorcycle. The garage owner rolled it out, and Frank sucked in his breath.

"Was it hidden in a barn when Hitler died?" Frank muttered. Still, beggars couldn't be choosers. After the old man filled the gas tank and gave him a road map, Frank took off.

Outside of town Frank opened his satchel and took out the receiver for the tracking unit. A loud blip sounded in his earphones when he aimed the aerial straight ahead.

Driving on with frequent checks, Frank stayed on the bus's trail. His quarry picked up a main road cutting across the island, and by the time Frank reached the Rügendamm— the half-mile causeway that connected the island with mainland Germany—the blips in Frank's ears were louder.

Together they headed southeast along the coast to a town called Greifswald. Then the bus turned due south. The highway they were on ended at Berlin.

"Welcome to Berlin!" Mr. Ducats's voice shattered Joe Hardy's uneasy dozing. The sun was setting, but Joe still turned to the window, eager for a glimpse of the city. He didn't know what he expected to see—stately stone houses, a palace maybe, or the classic columns of the Brandenburg Gate with its goddess on a chariot, reining in four wild horses.

Instead he looked out on drab concrete box housing. "This was the old regime's housing for workers," Ducats said.

"I've seen army barracks that were more inviting," Joe mumbled.

"Too bad, because you will spend the night in one of these apartments," Ducats said. "We were able to get the entire building very cheaply."

"Why am I not surprised?" Joe said quietly to Ilsa.

"You will be happy to know that this is your last stop," Ducats went on. "Tomorrow morning you will be aboard a plane heading for America."

Joe looked around. He saw mixed fear and joy from Cheng and Lu Wong, and from Fuat Dere. Ilsa's face was unreadable. Satisfaction beamed from the face of the man in the sunglasses. Greed shone in the eyes of the pimply youth. And Gustav Strular appeared to be deep in thought.

"You will share apartments," Ducats went on. "And, of course, you are not to leave the building once you enter. Get what rest you can. I warn you, your journey to America will not be comfortable."

Joe and Fuat Dere chose to share an apartment. They stowed their scanty gear in separate bedrooms. Then Joe stepped into the hallway to check the place out.

The building couldn't have been more than twenty-five years old. But when he looked in the stairwell, Joe found huge patches where the walls were literally crumbling away.

"It went up quickly and most likely will come down the same way," a voice said from behind Joe.

He turned to find Ilsa Khoo standing in the stairwell door. "Yeah," Joe agreed, "some things you just can't trust."

"Like me?" Ilsa went up a few steps on the next flight of stairs, then sat down. Her jade green eyes were on a level with Joe's. They looked at him steadily. "Joe," she whispered, "if I wanted to make trouble for you, you know how easy it would be. I haven't even asked why you joined this—this trip. Although I can guess."

"And I guess for you this little tour beats answering a lot of questions from the Swedish police," Joe said.

Ilsa's eyes flashed. "I'm only going along for one reason. Sooner or later this route will lead to whoever killed my father. I thought *you* might understand that."

Before Joe could say anything more, Ilsa rose to her feet and stalked off.

She headed down the hall, stepped into the apartment next to Joe's, and slammed the door.

A nasty laugh echoed off the naked concrete. Joe turned to see the scar-faced guard standing farther down the corridor, his arms full of food bags.

"How do you Americans say it?" Scar-face said. "You cannot get to first base with her." He laughed again, shaking his head. "Too bad we had to leave Sven in Copenhagen. He said he was getting somewhere with that one."

Wordlessly Joe took a sack of sandwiches in to share with Fuat Dere. He ate without gusto. All of a sudden Joe felt very, very tired.

He went to his room and dropped onto the bed, still fully clothed. For a while he stared at the ceiling, making pictures out of the various cracks. His eyes grew heavier and heavier until they closed.

Joe woke from a dreamless sleep to find the room pitch dark. He ran a dry tongue over still drier lips, blinking. What had wakened him up?

There seemed to be noise outside. Someone was yelling something like *"Eld!"*

Someone—it sounded like Ducats—yelled, *"Fuoco!"*

A woman screamed, and Joe dashed to the

door. He threw it open, and a wall of smoke entered the room.

Outside another of the multinational fugitives yelled, *"Feuer!"*

Now Joe knew the meaning of the strange words.

Fire!

Chapter

12

THE SMOKE filled the apartment with terrifying speed. Joe ran to Fuat Dere's room, only to find it empty. His next stop was the bathroom, where he soaked a threadbare towel in water and wrapped it around his face.

With some protection against the smoke Joe quickly checked the rest of the rooms for Fuat. He was nowhere.

Joe gave up and stepped out into the hallway. The smoke was worse, blinding his eyes and choking him.

What about Ilsa? he thought, groping his way to her apartment.

The door stood open. "Ilsa?" Joe called, then his body was racked with a fit of coughing. "Are you in there?"

He got no answer, and there was no way he could see her in all the smoke. Joe dropped to the floor, below the smoke level, and peered into the apartment. Crawling in, he conducted a quick search. No Ilsa.

The hallway was noticeably hotter when he crawled back outside. A dull, angry red glow seemed to emanate from the stairwell on the far side of the building.

Had anyone been quartered over there? Joe wondered. Where were the Wongs?

He realized the best way to find out was to get outside and count noses. Still on his knees, he scuttled for the other stairwell, the one where he and Ilsa had spoken earlier.

The smoke grew thicker as he worked his way down. Flames were so well established on the ground floor that Joe couldn't get to the front door.

Turning to a vacant apartment further from the fire, Joe kicked in the door, shut it behind him, then crawled through to the front room. He shoved up a window and climbed out—right into the arms of the scar-faced guard.

"Got you!" the man said. Joe was surprised at the enforcer's harassed expression.

"Who else have you got?" he asked.

"It's who we *haven't* got that makes the problem," Scar-face said, pushing Joe ahead of him. "In the first confusion several of you just ran off into the street."

"Who?" Joe began, but he was cut off as the scar-faced guard shoved him toward the Touristfahrt bus. Dawn was appearing, and Joe could clearly see Mr. Ducats scowling in the bus door. Two other enforcers flanked him. Inside, the group of fugitives had shrunk by more than half.

Ilsa sat very still, a jacket wrapped around her, just hugging herself.

The older man was alone, wearing trousers but no shirt. He had no sunglasses on.

Seeing the man's face for the first time, Joe thought he looked familiar. His face had been on television some time ago, on one of those wanted-criminal programs. The guy was some kind of white-collar criminal. Probably sneaking back to the U.S. to visit his money, Joe thought with a sour smile.

Behind him Joe heard Scar-face reporting. "I think he's the last to leave the building."

"No need to risk ourselves to find out," Ducats said. "We take it as given that the others are out on the streets."

He turned to his men. "Can one of you drive this thing? We shall have to drive around to find them. Otherwise—"

Joe thought of the Wongs wandering around a strange city. They had no money, probably hadn't even stopped to collect their few belongings. Joe felt a pang of sympathy. They *had* to find the couple.

He took the seat beside Ilsa and peered up into Ducats's face. He wasn't wearing the expression of a man trying to rescue people. No, his pudgy features had the hard cast of a businessman trying to decide whether or not to cut his losses.

If the cops picked up any of the people, they'd find out about the smuggling operation. Joe also realized with a sick sense of doom that they were all potential witnesses. Maybe Ducats would kill them all.

Scar-face got behind the wheel and started the bus. They found the Wongs about a block and a half away, sitting huddled and lost on the edge of the pavement. Lu Wong was crying.

"That leaves three," Ducats said grimly. "Strular, the Turk, and the kid."

A few blocks farther on they spotted the pimply-faced young man.

After he'd been gathered in, Ducats came to a decision. "Open the door," he told Scar-face. Then he turned to the other two guards. "Out," he said briefly. "You continue to search while we bring these to the depot."

Frank Hardy sat crouched over his motorcycle, taking yet another fix on his tracking device. His electronic surveillance had worked well enough, right until they'd reached Berlin. That was where Frank had made the sad discovery that multistory buildings interfered with the device's efficiency.

He'd been driving for hours trying to track the tourist bus. Now he'd done it. The blipping noise in his ears was almost deafening.

Frank looked down the block and saw the bus and his brother being shoved aboard. The bus took off, and Frank prepared to follow. Then he heard the cry for help.

Frank had paid no attention to the building where the bus was parked. All of his attention had been on catching up with Joe. Now he took in the smoke pouring out of the ground floor and the gray face peering down from the second-floor window. "Help!" the man cried in a choked voice. *"Hilfe!"*

Frank knew that was the same cry in German. "Hang on!" he called. As he came closer he recognized the man. It was the young Turk he'd seen outside Lea Kerk's office in Stockholm.

A quick glance told Frank that the front door was already blocked with flames. In fact, most of the first floor was ablaze. The Turk must have discovered that, fled to a second-floor apartment, and found himself trapped.

The question was, how could Frank get him out? The man was out of view. He'd apparently passed out. Frank didn't have much time.

He went to the corner of the building, noting that shoddy construction had left deep cracks and holes in the concrete. There seemed to be enough cracks and crevices here for him to climb.

He rested his fingers in a large crack overhead, tugged, and found the hold pretty solid. There was even an indentation in easy reach for a toehold. Frank worked his way up and soon found himself almost within reach of a second-floor window. The problem was, he'd have to jump sideways to get there.

Well, it's not all that far to the ground, he told himself. He leapt and for a sickening moment didn't think he could maintain a grip on the corroded window ledge. But he held on, clinging with an elbow as he levered the window up with his other arm.

Smoke greeted him as he crawled in. At last Frank got his bearings and discovered a body on the floor. Okay, Frank thought, here's the Turk. Now to concentrate on getting us out. The room was like an oven. Frank had an uncomfortable thought. If they stayed much longer, they might get baked to death.

He started examining the room's furnishings. There was no way he could carry an unconscious man down the way he'd come up. He needed to find some way to climb down. The bedspread would be okay as a do-it-yourself rope ladder, but what could he tie it to? The bed itself was too light.

In the end Frank wound up breaking the clothes rod out of the closet. It was wider than the window, so he could use it as the brace for his improvised ladder. He tied the spread to the rod, threw the other end of the spread to the ground below, and tried to revive the semiconscious Turk.

"We climb down together," Frank said as the man faced him with glazed eyes.

"It was the German—Strular," the young man said. "Couldn't sleep. Went into hall, heard noises. Saw Strular setting fire. Ran to stop—" The man's hand went to his head. "He hit me."

"Can you climb down on your own?" Frank asked.

The young man blinked his dark eyes. "Think so."

Frank helped the wobbly man out the window. Somehow the Turk made it to the ground below. A yell came from up the block, and Frank saw a burly man—one of the smugglers' guards, he realized—come running up.

"We thought the building was empty!" the guard cried as he yanked the sinking Turk upright. "Come on."

The Turk made feeble efforts to point to the window.

No, Frank thought, don't call attention to me.

The guard bundled the Turk off. After they were out of sight, Frank climbed down from the window—just in time.

He got on his motorcycle to follow the men and the Turk. They half dragged him to a deserted industrial area where Frank could see the tourist bus and a small truck. The bus passengers were being transferred to the back of the truck.

Ducats, the plump smuggler, closed the rear doors on the truck, sealing them into the windowless rear compartment. He locked the doors, then got in the cab. The van headed back toward Frank, who pretended to be fiddling with his engine. As soon as the van was past, Frank was back in the saddle, pursuing the truck.

They drove for about twelve miles, past signs that announced Schönefeld Flughafen. "Schonefeld Airport," Frank translated. "They're using the old East Berlin airport."

The airfield perimeter was surrounded by a chain-link fence topped with barbed wire. The truck went through a guarded security gate. Frank could only stop his cycle and watch through the fence. The truck didn't have far to go. It headed for a warehouse at the very edge of the field. Frank's eyes narrowed as he recognized the man standing in the loading bay door.

It was Karl Bremer.

Frank lost some time finding a secluded section of fencing to climb over. By the time he made it to the warehouse, the truck had been unloaded. Frank took cover behind the vehicle and peered around it.

Karl Bremer stood in the middle of the nearly empty warehouse, inspecting the bedraggled fugitives. He ran a muscular hand through his close-cropped hair, a frown on his heavy features.

"Everything has gone wrong with this run. In fact, everything has gone wrong since I had to leave Stockholm. The police and Interpol are after me. They've just about taken my house apart. I've been lucky to stay ahead of the law."

He glared at Ducats. "How much longer can I depend on that?" he demanded. "Can I trust our pipeline if you can't even bring these few miserable—"

Bremer cut off his tirade for an apologetic smile at Ilsa. "Of course, I don't include you in that description, my dear."

His expression turned nasty again as he continued. "You leave a guard behind in Copenhagen, get our Berlin safe house burned down, and even lose one client!"

"These things are not my fault," Ducats said defensively. "Berlin is our safest exit port, and our system here is foolproof."

"Even so, I wish to speak to the head office before we leave," Bremer said brusquely. "Where is a telephone?"

Ducats hastened to show Bremer to a partitioned-off cubicle as Frank sneaked inside. The muscular man stalked arrogantly after Ducats.

Ducats rushed back outside to put guards around the warehouse. Frank dashed along behind a low wall of crates that covered his route almost to the office wall. He risked crossing open space to climb a pile of the crates so he could look down into the office space.

Bremer was on the phone, a servile note creeping into his voice. "No, sir, of course I'm not trying to second-guess you. I realize that New York is your department, and that nothing can go wrong under your jurisdiction. I simply—"

He stopped speaking, apparently cut off by the person on the other end. "Yes, sir, I understand. It's just that this has been an extremely difficult operation. Ever since you ordered me to liquidate Khoo, we have had problems."

A sudden scraping noise took Frank's attention from Bremer, making him focus on the far wall of the office. Someone had climbed boxes on that side and was also peering down into the room. Frank froze as he recognized Ilsa Khoo.

Her face was twisted in an expression of rage.

If looks could kill, Frank thought, Bremer would be dead right now.

Chapter

13

"YES, SIR," Karl Bremer went on, "the cleanup is almost over. We've closed down the Stockholm operation, eliminated all records, and liquidated the most dangerous witnesses."

Across the office Frank Hardy saw Ilsa Khoo's eyes flash.

"I'm also bringing the daughter. She has information that Khoo never committed to records. Valuable information, she assures me. After we debrief her . . . Yes, sir. I understand perfectly. Very good. Yes, in a few hours." Bremer hung up the phone, and Ilsa quickly disappeared from her vantage point atop the boxes. Frank waited a moment or two, then climbed down to take cover behind the office wall.

"Are the containers ready?" Bremer asked.

"All here," Ducats said, rejoining him and indicating the row of cartons Frank had used as cover to make his way to the office. The chubby man picked up a crowbar and opened the first box in the line, revealing a padded interior, oxygen tanks, even a self-contained waste unit.

"Your personal cabins for the America trip," Ducats informed the other travelers, who had now gathered around. "They may be a little more cramped than tourist class, but they are much more private. More protected from prying eyes."

As Ducats spoke the guards got to work opening the other crates. Karl Bremer carefully inspected them all, then chose the largest box, but didn't get in yet. Ilsa Khoo was placed in the next container, then the older fugitive, followed by the pimply-faced traveler.

The young couple clung together till the last moment. Guards were already sealing the crates, nailing them shut, when Ducats took the woman by the arm and led her to her container.

"We need only two more," Ducats said. "The container for Herr Strular will be left for the next shipment."

Frank took advantage of the couple's goodbyes to sneak to a side entrance hidden by the office walls. As he quietly stepped out of the warehouse, he spotted a figure on foot heading toward him from the main terminal buildings. Ducking behind more shipping crates, Frank observed the man's progress. The stranger wore a trench coat and was carefully carrying some sort of satchel.

As he drew nearer Joe recognized the newcomer. It was Gustav Strular, the German Joe had told him about.

The small man hurried along just like a commuter worried about missing his train. Frank waited until Strular had almost reached the warehouse before he stepped into sight. A crazy idea had taken root in his mind.

Strular recoiled at Frank's sudden appearance, then smiled. *"Ach.* Security, yes?"

Frank glanced down at his grubby clothes. Yes, he decided, he probably looked like one of the uglies the smuggling ring hired as enforcers.

"I am Gustav Strular," the German informed Frank briskly. "I am supposed to be with the group leaving for America. We became separated during a fire."

Strular smirked, adding in a confidential tone, "Not that I mind. It gave me a chance to pick up my retirement fund."

He hefted the satchel he carried. "This holds the results of twenty-five years of prudent investment—all in very transportable form."

Strular went to move past Frank, but Frank stepped into his path. "I'm surprised you took so long to recover your investments."

The German man stopped and stared. "The end of the government came very quickly. I was not able—"

"You weren't able to leave with all your ill-gotten gains," Frank finished for him. "So when you learned you'd be back in Berlin, you set a fire in the safe house to cover your tracks while you gathered your loot."

Strular did an unconvincing job of acting shocked. "I would never—"

"The Turk lived. He told us everything."

That took the wind out of Strular's sails. His watery eyes narrowed. "Would you be interested in a small commission for an extra job? An American boy in our group—I want him dead. I will pay the boy's passage—dead or alive. I would just prefer him dead."

A grim smile came to Frank's lips as he heard this proposal. "I don't think you have enough in that satchel to pay me," he told Strular. "You see, that American is my brother."

Strular staggered back in shock. Then his face went hard, and he shoved his hand into his coat.

Frank moved with the speed of a striking

snake. His left leg snapped out in a high kick, smashing into Strular's hand while the German was still drawing the gun from an underarm holster.

Strular howled with pain and bent over. His hand emerged from under his coat empty, but the gun didn't drop to the ground.

Face twisted, Strular attacked with his only other weapon, the heavy satchel, swinging it at Frank's head. Frank ducked, and the bag only grazed his temple.

Strular took advantage of his opponent's off-balance position to try to dig out his gun again.

This time Frank didn't fool around with trying to disarm him. His leg flew out in a roundhouse kick, connecting solidly with Strular's chin. The man went down like a felled tree.

His satchel flew up in a high arc and landed with a rattling thump. Frank left the unconscious German and went to examine the bag. When he opened it he gasped. The satchel was filled with gems!

Frank sealed the bag over the glittering hoard, slipped it under his arm, and strode around to the front of the warehouse. Two guards moved to intercept him. "I'm from Strular," Frank told them.

One guard, a burly guy with a scar down his face, said, "Bring him to Ducats."

Frank walked inside to find Karl Bremer

and another guard covering him with pistols. "If you can't satisfy me about how you know of Strular and our presence here, you won't leave alive," Bremer said.

"I came to Germany with the U.S. Army and stayed on, as they say, 'without official leave,' " Frank said coolly. "Strular used me for odd jobs. When old Gustav left Germany I was supposed to guard his stash. I got a message to meet him here. When I arrived I discovered he intended to retire me as his pension guardian—permanently. I nailed him first. Since he'd told me about this operation, I decided to take his place."

"The question is, can you pay for your passage?" Bremer asked.

"Let me show you something," Frank said, opening the bag. "And do me a favor, don't shoot, okay?"

He slowly put his hand in the bag and drew out a handful of jewels. Total silence reigned in the warehouse as the smugglers stared in complete disbelief.

"I take it this will handle my fare," Frank said.

"Open Strular's container," Bremer ordered. "We have a replacement."

A muffled cry came from the warehouse entrance. Frank turned—and froze. Half leaning, half sagging against the scar-faced guard was Gustav Strular.

The small man's pale blue eyes glittered with hate as he pointed at Frank and the jewels he held outstretched. *"Dee-uh!"* Strular cried, his other hand gripping his jaw.

"What is he saying?" Bremer demanded angrily.

Scar-face shook his head. "I can't make out anything he says."

Frank suddenly understood. *I must have broken the guy's jaw. He can't pronounce anything!*

What could Strular have been trying to communicate? *Dee-uh.* Of course—the German word for thief, *Dieb.*

Infuriated, Strular broke into an explosion of incoherent sounds. Still clutching his injured jaw, the German continued to point at Frank, glaring vengeance.

"Shee-own!" Strular cried, his face twisted with pain and fury. He turned desperately from Bremer to the scar-faced guard. *"Shee-own!"* he said again, his voice rising in hysteria.

Frank stood blank-faced. Apparently, he was the only one in the room who had managed to decode Strular's mangled German. He was trying to say *Spion,* his mother tongue's word for "spy."

Bremer shook his head in annoyance, then turned to Frank. "Is this your doing?"

Frank shrugged. "I think I mentioned we

had a little disagreement. He thought his safety lay in cheating me out of my share of the loot.''

Another outraged hoot came from Strular, but Frank went on with his story. "So I popped him one and left while he was out cold.'' Frank tried to look modest. "Looks like I managed to give him a real shot.''

Bremer and the guards laughed.

Perhaps that persuaded Strular that he couldn't convince the smugglers. The German stopped muttering, pushed himself away from the guard supporting him, and stabbed a hand under his coat.

Before Strular could get his gun out, however, the scar-faced guard moved with brutal efficiency. His thick left arm applied a choke hold to Strular's neck, which must have been excruciating for a man with a broken jaw. Scar-face grabbed Strular's wrist and yanked his arm out of the coat with a crushing grip. Frank could hear bones grinding in Strular's wrist.

The gun clattered to the concrete floor.

"Another thing,'' Scar-face said. "When I picked up the Turk, he said this one started the fire.''

Bremer turned to Ducats and the other guards. "Well, gentlemen, I think Herr Strular has proven himself a liability. I suggest we go with his replacement.''

123

The guards finished opening the final container, and Frank was ushered in. He sat down and strapped himself into the padded surface, keeping the satchel of gems in his lap.

"Get a move on," Ducats instructed his people. "Our customs man will be here soon, and so will the cargo handlers."

Frank slipped the oxygen mask over his face as the guards fit the container cover in place.

The last thing Frank saw was Gustav Strular being dragged off by a pair of brawny guards. The German's voice grew shriller as he babbled incoherently.

The noise was cut off as the lid was sealed.

Now that he was unseen, Frank reached into his pocket, pulling out a small radio set with earphones. He might be blind, but thanks to one of Rutger Linska's tiny bugs tossed on the warehouse floor, he wasn't deaf.

Not that Frank could hear very much. Mainly what he caught was the pounding of hammers nailing him in.

Then a single, sharp sound reverberated through the building.

Frank recognized it immediately.

It was a gunshot.

Chapter

14

As Frank sat in his dark little container a chilling thought ran through his mind. These guys really don't kid around. They've got just one answer to any kind of problem—put a bullet in its brain.

The echoes of the shot had hardly died away before Karl Bremer's voice rang out. "Clear away that mess." His tone was almost bored. "Our guests will be here in a moment, and I have yet to be sealed in."

Through his bug Frank heard the noises of hurried movement and scuffling. Then came another siege of nailing.

"All sealed," a guard reported.

"And Strular?" Ducats's voice made it sound as if disposing of dead bodies was all in a normal day's work.

"We put him in an empty crate back by the office." Frank heard the voice of the scar-faced guard, sounding equally undisturbed.

Things became quiet for a few minutes. Then came a flurry of activity as Frank heard a vehicle pull up to the warehouse. A new voice, accented in German, joined with Ducats's.

"Here are your customs forms, *mein Herr,* all approved."

Frank heard the rustle of papers. "Very good," Ducats said. "You have done very well indeed." His words were accompanied by a papery slapping noise. Frank could just imagine a money-filled envelope thudding into the bribed customs official's palm.

Then came more rustling. *"Mein Herr,* you are more than generous for my small services." The corrupt official's voice sounded downright oily.

A sharp rap sounded through Frank's container as the corrupt official thumped it on the side. "It is good the American immigration people only concern themselves with passenger planes. No one would expect cargo to get up and walk, eh?"

Ducats's voice became very cold. "I am sure you have no need to concern yourself with our cargo. The customs forms you just signed specify it as chinaware, and very fragile. I don't see where this matter concerns you anymore."

"*Ach, nein, mein Herr.*" The corrupt German's voice became even oilier. He obviously didn't want to annoy the man who paid him so well. "It was just an idle comment. A compliment, even. No other operation has the technical expertise to transport, uh, cargo like this on such a scale."

"Idle compliments can lead to idle talk," Ducats said.

"Oh, *nein, nein,* no, I would never speak to anyone about such things. I was just talking to you, now, here between ourselves."

The German sounded scared. Frank wondered how much worse the man would sound if he knew just how ruthless the Phoenix smugglers really were. He'd fall apart if he saw what had happened to Gustav Strular, Frank thought.

"Here, sir," the German went on. "I brought these in case they might be useful on the other end. Customs seals." The voice became even more ingratiating. "To make your cargo all the more official."

"Interesting," Ducats said. "You may have earned yourself a bonus, my friend."

The voices in Frank's ears faded as Ducats moved away, apparently followed by the babbling German.

Again, silence in the warehouse. And again

a vehicle arrived. Then came the sound of numerous loud voices all talking in German, and the scrape and thump of boxes being moved.

This must be the cargo crew, Frank realized. In a moment Frank was tumbled as the container he occupied was unceremoniously hauled around. He had already noticed that the crates were all marked Fragile and had large arrows indicating which end was up.

I hope these guys pay attention to it, Frank thought. I'd hate to make this trip standing on my head.

Just as Frank's container was dumped onto the cargo carrier an unbearably loud *skkkrrrrr-kkkkk!* came over his earphones. Frank tore the phones off. By sheer bad luck, one of the workers must have stepped right on his bug.

Frank massaged his pounding temples. It didn't make much difference, he supposed. Once they were out of the warehouse he'd lose his audio link to the outside world anyway. Frank was jostled as the cargo carrier pulled out of the warehouse.

Well, Frank thought, we're on our way.

A good eight hours later Joe Hardy heard the welcome sound of crowbars attacking the container that surrounded him. He'd spent the entire trip across the Atlantic in the dark, wondering where he was. His only guide had been the steady throbbing of the cargo plane's en-

gines. When they'd swept down to land Joe
had had the nightmarish vision that they were
going to crash.

To pass the time in the dark, Joe had gone
back over the entire case. He and Frank had
come a long way from that first meeting in
Congressman Alladyce's office with the representative and Ethan Daly, the top customs
man. They had also wound up fighting a lot
more than animal smugglers.

Joe honestly couldn't remember a more gru-
eling case for him and Frank, and not just in
terms of sleepless nights and physical hurt.
There had been the emotional pain of thinking
that their father had been killed. But now,
with luck, one of them might catch up with
Fenton Hardy. Perhaps they'd even get a shot
at the head of the Phoenix operation. Then
the lid of the crate was cracked open, and Joe
blinked at what to him seemed like a terrible
glare.

As his eyes slowly got used to the light he
realized it was pretty dim, actually. He released the straps that held him in place, and
a couple of brawny arms assisted him in his
first tottering steps out of the crate.

Cramped from his long confinement, Joe
moved like an old man. He gazed around at
his surroundings, taking a deep breath of
musty air. It made a great change from the
oxygen bottle.

For a moment, looking at gray warehouse walls, he wondered if he'd gone anywhere at all.

But no, this was a different warehouse. The German place hadn't had that calendar on the wall. And outside the doors . . .

The Phoenix hangar seemed nearly at the perimeter of the airport. Again there was a chain-link fence. But beyond were small houses with green yards. This was Queens, New York, U.S.A. Joe was at JFK International Airport.

"America!" Ilsa Khoo said, emerging from her shell to join Joe. She tried to flex some life into her cramped limbs. "Are you all right?" she asked.

"I didn't think much of the in-flight movie," he told her with a grin.

Then she and Joe were reminded of how they'd gotten there.

"Well, I'll be dipped!" a loud voice said.

They turned to see a big guy with greasy hair advancing on them. One of his hands held a clipboard, the other a MAC-10 submachine gun. Tossing the board with a clatter on top of a crate, the man stared openly at Ilsa, admiring her.

The guard smiled at her and turned to help the others out.

Joe was amazed at how quickly the unpacking process was handled. In moments almost all of the travelers were out of their containers, and a crew was removing the shipping labels and slapping them onto other crates. Legitimate cargo, Joe guessed.

The empty padded boxes disappeared into a storage bay packed with identical-looking crates. Soon, any trace of the illegals and their mode of transport would be well hidden.

Cheng and Lu Wong emerged from their boxes to stand at the warehouse doors, eyes shining as they took in their promised land. The pimply-faced youth and the white-collar criminal were released next, both of them groaning and complaining about the trip. Fuat Dere was next out. The young Turkish man shook his head as he also stared out the door. "I never thought I would make it," he muttered.

Then there was only one crate left. "That's odd," Ilsa said to Joe. "You'd think that Karl Bremer would have been the first to be unpacked."

Joe shrugged. "Maybe they got their signals switched. Or maybe it's an empty, the one Strular was supposed to ride in."

But when the lid was wedged off it revealed neither emptiness nor Gustav Strular, but Frank Hardy!

Joe knew he had to be gaping as he stared at his brother. A storm of mixed emotions passed through him. Joe felt shock, delight, relief that Frank was okay, and most of all, amazement. How had his older brother managed to switch places with the nasty Mr. Strudel?

Glancing over at Ilsa Khoo, Joe noted that she looked just as dumbfounded as he did.

Frank noticed their expressions and grinned. "Hey," he said, "when you've got a good travel agent, all things are possible."

The reunion was interrupted by the ugly *snick* of a gun safety being thumbed off.

"Hey, pal," the greasy-haired guard said grimly. "My listing says a skinny bald guy is supposed to come out of that box. You ain't bald, and you ain't skinny."

The guard's submachine gun was leveled mere inches from Frank's chest. "So you're gonna be dead, spy!"

Chapter

15

FRANK HARDY DIDN'T ARGUE. He knew words couldn't stop a machine gun that emptied a thirty-round clip in less than a second. Only action would do.

The gun had made the guard too confident. He was much too close. Frank pivoted his body, smashing his open hand against the MAC-10. The gun no longer covered him. Then Frank spun back around the way he'd come, raising his arm this time. His elbow made a solid connection with the guard's jaw.

The guy dropped, but even as he was falling Frank's left hand plucked the submachine gun from the guard's nerveless grasp. Frank moved so a crate protected his back, covering the whole room with the MAC-10. In the space of a few heartbeats he'd turned the situation around.

As the adrenaline wore off his muscles protested painfully from being stretched so soon after leaving the cramped confines of the box. Frank paid no attention. He had to play this out.

"I don't care what it said on that guy's list," Frank said in a rough voice. "I'm on this run fair and square. You just ask Mr. Bremer. He'll tell you."

By now the other guards had pulled themselves together and were advancing. Several had drawn weapons. Frank panned the gun around, and they stopped in their tracks. "Just back off, all of you," Frank said. He glared at Joe. "You, too, pal. You and the pretty girl."

Both Joe's and Ilsa's eyebrows rose, but they played along, stepping back with everyone else.

"What is going on here?"

Karl Bremer appeared in the door of the warehouse. Frank noticed that he had already shaved and changed his clothes. The big man must have been first out of the box.

One of the guards said, "This guy knocked out Greasy Charlie and took his gun. He's not on the cargo list, and Charlie was going to waste him."

"Subordinates," Bremer muttered. "Why are there never enough intelligent ones?"

He turned to take in the entire crew. "This man replaced the person on the master list at the last minute. He's a special cargo, paying a bonus rate. Speaking of which—"

Bremer stepped forward, and the guards put away their guns. Frank dropped Greasy Charlie's MAC-10 and picked up Gustav Strular's satchel from where he'd dropped it to take care of the guard. He opened the bag, dug out a fistful of gems, and dropped them into Bremer's palm.

Hungry looks shot among the smugglers as they went off to evaluate the loot.

Soon enough, however, Bremer and his henchmen were back. "We will now move you from the airport to safe houses," Bremer announced. "This is the best time, since there is a shift change of airport staff. It will require a small disguise."

The guards went among the travelers, distributing coveralls.

Frank and Joe exchanged grimly amused glances. After all, the last time they'd worn coveralls to get to a safe house, the place had been firebombed.

After everyone, including the guards, Bremer, and the still-groggy Greasy Charlie, had donned the disguises, they were split up for travel.

The two fugitives who had joined the group with Ilsa rode in a car with two guards. The rest of the group crowded into a van with bus seats. Leaving the airport presented no problems. The driver swung onto an access road, joined the flow of airport traffic, and soon was threading a route along the Belt Parkway.

Their destination turned out to be a derelict building near the Brooklyn Bridge. As Frank and Joe were shepherded up the stoop they could actually see the towers of the bridge rising in the near distance. Ahead of them spread the skyline of downtown Manhattan.

Cheng Wong and his wife, Lu, took in the view with excited gazes. "Soon," Cheng promised his wife, squeezing her hands. "Soon it will be ours."

"Right," a revived Greasy Charlie told them. "Just as soon as you pay your fare."

Entering the safe house, Frank and Joe discovered that payment could be a real problem for some of the illegal aliens. Until the smugglers received their money, the travelers would be kept as prisoners. Dozens of people were penned up in the decrepit building, sleeping wherever they could find an empty room.

"I don't suppose either of you lads would have a ciggie," a man with a sandy beard and a thick Australian accent asked them.

"Sorry," Frank said.

"Gone three weeks without a decent

smoke." The man shook his head. "When I think that I came to this country first all nice and legal, it makes me want to spit."

"What happened?" Joe wanted to know.

"Had a brush with the law, and they deported me. But I thought I was Jack the lad, and I'd sneak back in. Problem is, my old mates haven't come up with the money for me yet, so I'm rotting in this dump."

"One of the guards said that I wouldn't have to stay here if I didn't want to," Frank said.

"Sure, if you've got the cash to stay at the Smuggler's Arms," the Australian man said. "That's what we call it around here. It's a nice little house just down the road here, done up like a posh hotel."

The boys exchanged glances. So there were two places to check out if they wanted to find their father. They continued to go over the safe house until a suspicious Greasy Charlie barged past, then confronted them at the top stairwell.

"What are you two up to, anyway?" the guard demanded. "I been following you around, and it's like you're searching for something in here. Something—or *someone*."

"Charlie!" A light female voice floated up the stairs.

They turned to see Ilsa Khoo climbing up toward them. "There you are!" she said, a flirtatious note in her voice. She was on the top step now, looking boldly up into Greasy Charlie's eyes. "Are you feeling better now?" Ilsa purred.

"Babe, right now I feel great," the guard assured her, taking her arm and heading back downstairs.

From the look on Joe's face, Frank could tell that something must have been going on between his kid brother and Ilsa since Copenhagen. Joe looked as if he couldn't believe she'd pick this greasy slob over him. His jaw tightened, and his hands clenched into fists as he watched them walk off.

"She ain't worth picking a fight over," a hoarse voice from down the hall assured them. The boys watched as a lanky figure shuffled toward them, finally entering the wan pool of light in the stairwell.

The man's hair was askew, and he had at least a week's growth of beard. "Sorry, pal, we don't have any cig—" Frank's voice cut off. It had taken a moment, but now he recognized the scarecrow who stood before them.

It was Fenton Hardy.

"Don't smoke, myself," Fenton said, his eyes flashing a warning. "I was just lookin' for some company."

The boys smothered their joy at finding their father. They were in the midst of enemies. If he wanted them to act like strangers, they'd play along.

Fenton led them away from the landing and down the hall, where another feeble pool of half light fell from a dim ceiling bulb. "This is a good place to crash," he went on in his hoarse voice. "Nobody comes up this high. Guess they don't like to climb the stairs. See? Lots of rooms."

He opened a door. "This one's mine."

They stepped in, and suddenly Fenton's voice became normal, if softer than usual. "We should be all right now, out of earshot from the stairway. I haven't found any listening devices in this dump."

"Dad—" Frank and Joe both whispered. Frank didn't know about his brother, but he was having a hard time keeping the moisture out of his eyes.

"I know, boys, I know. It must have seemed like a cruel trick, letting you and your mother think I'd died in Mombasa. But I had to do it."

Fenton Hardy looked grim. "If the other side thought I was dead, it gave me a much better chance to infiltrate. And hard as it was to do, I needed your genuine grief to convince them. I had other reasons, too."

He stared at the boys. "How did you find me?"

Frank quickly explained about finding the

list of smuggling clients in Bremer's office. "As soon as we saw the name Ezra Collig, we knew we had to track you down." He shook his head. "Forget that. How did you survive that bomb blast in Mombasa?"

"I heard you two shout a warning and bailed out a rear window into the water just as the bomb went off."

Fenton was silent for a moment, looking at the boys.

"I was swimming back when a whole lot of little things came together for me—the other reason to disappear. Instead of announcing my escape, I dived under a pier and left myself for dead."

Frank looked at his father with a rude suspicion. "You didn't trust anybody on our side anymore, did you?"

"I'd trust you boys with my life," Fenton said. "That's why I used Collig's name when I went into the smuggling pipeline. I knew that if you came across it, you'd come after me."

His face hardened. "But I'm catching a smell of rot in this investigation. And it's coming from the very top."

Frank nodded. "We know someone is leaking information to the Phoenix ring. They gave away the safe house where we were supposed to be staying, and the place got firebombed."

"It's worse than that, I'm afraid." Fenton reached into his rumpled clothes and came out with several sheets of paper. "I want you boys out of here before the balloon goes up. I also need your help. Get these messages to—"

"I'm afraid there's no outgoing mail, Fenton," a voice came from the hallway. Its menace was underscored by the sharp *snick* of bullets being engaged in guns.

But only one person stepped into the circle of pale yellow light thrown by the overhead bulb.

Frank's stomach went tight as he recognized the man. It was Assistant Commissioner Ethan Daly. "I'm also afraid I really can't let you tear my whole operation apart," Daly said.

"So I was right," Fenton Hardy said sorrowfully. "You are the big cheese behind this whole dirty business."

"It's good to see you, too, Fenton," Daly said, a grim smile playing across his features, "and a pleasure to see your fine young sons again. But I'm afraid we'll have to cut this little reunion short. Regrettable, but you know how bloodthirsty my associates are."

Three guards stepped into the doorway. All carried guns.

"And in this case," Daly went on, "I think they'd be right to kill you."

Chapter

16

"OH," ETHAN DALY SAID. "Let me add one more member to this party."

Ilsa Khoo appeared in the doorway with Greasy Charlie and his trusty MAC-10.

"I don't know how you did it," Daly said to the boys. "How could you turn my own partner's daughter against me?"

"You pig!" Ilsa Khoo spat. "I know you had my father killed. He always kept me out of his business, and now I know why. But I pretended to Bremer that I had information. The only reason I went along with him was to find you." She took a deep breath. "When your guard stopped the boys, I led him away. I knew that whatever they were searching for would hurt you."

Her green eyes glittered. "And that's the one thing I want most in this world."

In spite of the deep trouble they were in, happiness flowed through Joe Hardy. Ilsa *was* one of the good guys!

"Well, I'm sorry to disappoint you, Miss Khoo. But Charlie here isn't as dumb as he looks. And sorry, Fenton, I've got a full dossier on you. I knew about your connection with Ezra Collig. The name didn't fool me."

He shook his head in reluctant admiration. "You boys are quite amazing. Not only did you smash two of my most profitable operations, but you infiltrated the third."

Daly glanced at them. "You could have quite a career if you joined up with me. You know the old saying 'It takes a thief to catch a thief'? Well, the opposite is true. It takes a cop or detective to make a great crook. I'm living proof."

"Certainly, you knew where your agency would be concentrating," Fenton said.

"I knew where *all* the law-enforcement agencies were working," Daly corrected him. "After all, I'm in charge of coordinating our efforts."

"So it was easy to coordinate things out of your way," Joe said.

"And having combated smugglers for years, you knew all the tricks," Frank added.

THE HARDY BOYS CASEFILES

Daly nodded as if he were acknowledging compliments.

"You probably even knew which scum you could hire," Fenton went on.

"Better than that," Daly said, "I could investigate people to see if they were corrupt or if they could be corrupted. I knew which respectable business types could be turned to my purpose and which officials could be persuaded to turn a blind eye. When I organized Phoenix Enterprises through Lyle Banner, I designed it to be the industry leader in smuggling."

"Well, I'm glad we were able to wreck your little empire," Joe said.

"Oh, you hurt me," Daly admitted. "You cost me a lot. But I'll rebuild, and you won't be around to stop me. We're going to see to that right now."

"You're just going to blow us away up here?" Joe asked in disbelief.

"Why not?" Daly said. "No one in this neighborhood will investigate. The only people who'll hear are the illegals downstairs. And—well, they don't know it yet, but they're all going to die. The Phoenix operation has been compromised, so I'm going to shut it— and them—down. A name change, some new partners, and Phoenix Enterprises will be reborn and in business again."

His face hardened. "But I think this is

enough discussion. Charlie, boys, take care of them.''

The enforcers raised their guns, smiling.

At the exact moment the downstairs doors and windows were smashed in. Loudspeakers bellowed, "This is the police! Freeze!" The illegal aliens charged up the stairs then, too.

Greasy Charlie pushed through the guards at the doorway, intending to spray the hallway and the illegals with bullets.

But Charlie was too late. He got into position just in time to be clubbed down by Fuat Dere, who brandished a broken chair leg. "I knew something was up when they grabbed Ilsa," the young Turk yelled. "They're not going to kill us!"

Ilsa, meanwhile, had taken advantage of the commotion. She was the closest to the armed men. As Charlie pushed through, she shoved off in a high leap, spearing one guard with an outthrust leg while chopping another down with a slash of her arm.

Joe, Frank, and Fenton were right behind her, turning what could have been a gunfight into a hand-to-hand melee instead.

Joe watched as a determined-looking Lu Wong used a heavy frying pan to slug smugglers.

Fenton Hardy deftly twisted an automatic pistol right out of a guard's hand. Then, while the man gawked at him, Fenton bopped him on the head with the butt of the gun.

Ethan Daly, roaring like an animal, tore a gun out from under his jacket. Frank Hardy latched onto Daly's gun hand, trying for an arm lock while the customs man thrashed to get free.

Joe was moving to his brother's aid when Greasy Charlie suddenly erupted from the middle of the tangle, aiming his machine gun straight at Joe.

Then another body sailed from the confused welter of people. It was Ilsa Khoo, aiming a karate punch straight at Charlie's head.

The outstretched knuckles of her fist caught the guard right in the temple. Joe could have sworn he saw Charlie's eyes cross as he toppled.

Ilsa grinned and shook her hand. "Oooh, I wanted to get him," she said.

Meanwhile, Ethan Daly and Frank had stumbled into the more open space of Fenton Hardy's room as they struggled. Now Daly clawed his gun loose from Frank's hold and tried to turn his weapon on the elder Hardy.

Joe had only two steps to reach them, but he managed to put a lot of momentum into them as he grabbed Daly by the shoulder and turned him around. His fist came up in a perfect right cross, and Daly went down.

A tidal wave of blue uniforms came storming up the stairs, ending the fight.

Later, as the combined task force of police, immigration, and customs officers sorted things out, Fenton Hardy explained their rescue.

"I used the last of my funds bribing people to send a coded message to Sam Peterson, here."

The tall, powerfully built man standing by Fenton Hardy smiled. "Hello, boys," he said.

Both Frank and Joe knew him as Chief Peterson of the New York City Police Department. He and Fenton had served together on the streets back when Mr. Hardy had been with the New York force.

Fenton shook his head. "I figured it wouldn't be easy getting illegal aliens to contact the chief of the NYPD, but it's amazing what a hundred-dollar bill will do for some people."

Frank laughed. "Or even a handful of them."

Sam Peterson laughed, too. "Believe it or not, three people passed the message along. Based on the information, I arranged for a raid on this house with trustworthy members of INS and Customs, avoiding Daly, whom your father suspected."

"Well, you came just at the right moment," Frank said. His face sobered as he watched the people being led away. "What will happen to all the illegals?"

"That's up to the Immigration people, and maybe the courts," Peterson said.

"I'd like to put in a word for the Wongs and for Fuat Dere," Joe said. "We wouldn't have made it without them."

"I'm sure it wouldn't hurt," Fenton Hardy said.

At least one of the illegals wouldn't be shipped off immediately—Ilsa Khoo. She stood with a police medic, her hand in a plastic bag of ice.

"What happened?" Joe asked, rushing over.

"Either I didn't practice that punch right, or Greasy Charlie has a very thick head," Ilsa said, grimacing in pain. "I think I broke my hand."

"You were real impressive in that fight," Joe told her.

"My father taught me martial arts," Ilsa admitted. "But it's amazing how some guys respond when they learn you can break their arms."

Joe grinned. "Oh, I'd never let a little thing like that stop me. Not if I really wanted to go out with a person."

Ilsa's green eyes locked on his. "I wish things had been different, Joe. But I guess we both had secrets we couldn't let each other know."

"At least they're all out in the open now," Joe said. "I can see why you went off with Charlie. Now if I can only figure out what you saw in Sven, to sneak off dancing with him."

"You knew about that?" Ilsa's cheeks turned red. "I could see he was interested in me, so I decided to try to get information out of him."

"Yeah? Well, I'm glad Frank decked him in Copenhagen," Joe declared.

That made her laugh.

"But enough about the past," Joe said. "What about the future?"

"They'll want me as a witness against Daly and Phoenix Enterprises," Ilsa said quietly. "My mother had a sister, and I've always gotten on well with her. So I'll live with my aunt and uncle." She tried to smile at Joe and failed. "I'm sorry Stockholm is so far away."

"We still may have some time together in New York," Joe said. "And after that, well, there are airplanes. At least I won't have to smuggle myself back. Don't be surprised if I turn up in your hometown again."

Ilsa grinned, grabbed Joe's hand, and winced. Returning her hand to the ice bag again, she shook her head. "Nothing you do would surprise me, Joe Hardy."

Frank came over. "Chief Peterson has offered us a car to go over to his office. He'll still be here for a while, tying things up."

"Sounds like I've got to go," Joe said to Ilsa.

"Be seeing you," she said.

"Bet on it," Joe promised.

The trip across the Brooklyn Bridge passed in contented silence. Neither Fenton nor the boys wanted to break the spell of being together again.

Finally, however, Fenton spoke. "You did an outstanding job on this case, in spite of some tough curves that I threw at you. I want you to know I'm very proud."

"All we can say is that we're glad you're still around," Frank said.

"You got it," Joe agreed. "When we thought you were gone . . ." A shudder passed through him. "I never want that feeling again."

Fenton nodded, and they rode on in silence for a moment. "We'll have to call your mother right away, especially before we head home. I think she should tell your aunt Gertrude that I'm alive. Otherwise, I'll be greeted as a ghost." Frank and Joe both broke into laughter at the picture that conjured up.

"Right, Dad," Joe said. "We wouldn't want Aunt Gertrude thinking you're a ghost."

Frank and Joe's next case:

The Hardys have agreed to sail a friend's yacht from the island of Saint Martin to the coast of Florida. But sinister winds are blowing across the Caribbean, and the brothers' voyage is about to take a deadly detour. In the middle of the night, a 5,000-ton cargo ship appears out of the darkness and nearly sends the yacht—and the boys—to the bottom of the sea.

When Frank and Joe investigate, they discover that the freighter's crew is missing and that they've landed in a shipload of trouble. The ship's secret cargo may have incited a mutiny and may soon ignite the violent overthrow of an island nation. From Puerto Rico to Panama, the boys pursue a gang of black marketeers willing to sell anything—including human life—for a price . . . in *Lethal Cargo,* Case #67 in The Hardy Boys Casefiles™.

Together for the first time!

The Hardys' sleuthing skills join with Tom Swift's inventive genius in a pulse-pounding new breed of adventure.

A
HARDY BOYS
AND
TOM SWIFT
ULTRA THRILLER™

TIME BOMB

A twist in time . . . A twisted mind . . .
A terrifying twist of fate for Frank
and Joe and Tom!

A dream that has long fired the human imagination has become a reality: time travel. But as Tom Swift and the Hardy boys are about to discover, the dream can become a nightmare in the blink of an eye. An attack force of techno-thugs, under the command of the evil genius, the Black Dragon, has seized control of a top-secret time-warp trigger!

Frank, Joe, and Tom leap into battle. But whether chasing asteroids or dodging dinosaurs, they know they haven't a moment to lose. They must stop the Dragon before he carries out his final threat: turning the time machine into the ultimate doomsday device!

Turn the page for your very special preview of . . .

TIME BOMB

"Detectors ready, Rob?" Tom Swift asked his robot assistant. "We have cosmic rays incoming in less than fifteen seconds."

The young, blond inventor gestured at the array of particle detectors that spread along the ridge they stood on.

Rob's glowing eyes gazed into the California desert sky. "Why did we power all this up so far in advance of the particle stream?"

"I want to catch some particles coming *ahead* of the rush," Tom explained.

"But cosmic rays move at the speed of light."

"Tachyons move faster," Tom said. "They'll show up twenty milliseconds before anything else."

"If they exist," Rob pointed out.

"In theory they do," Tom said. "Now we'll see if the universe is a democracy or a dictatorship."

"You've lost me, Tom," Rob said.

Tom's lean face lit up with a grin, and his deep-set blue eyes twinkled. "Either everything that's possible is allowed to happen—or everything possible *must* happen."

Rob read the data flying along the computer linkup. "I've picked up several particle anomalies in advance of the air shower created by the cosmic ray collisions."

The robot was silent for a moment. "It's as if the tachyons arrived *before* those collisions. Does that mean they traveled through time?"

Tom shrugged. "We all travel through time, Rob. What makes tachyons interesting is that they move in the opposite direction from us—"

The gleaming robot suddenly interrupted. "You've got a phone call."

Tom stared. "What?"

"It's a new improvement I was trying out, building your portable phone into my circuits. Just talk. My sensors will pick up."

A second later, Tom Swift, Sr.'s voice came through Rob's speakers. "Tom, are you there? I'd like you to come to my office. A rather interesting package has arrived."

"We're on our way." Tom and Rob started down the side of the ridge, to the van parked on the road below. They drove through the hills until they arrived at Swift Enterprises and made their way to Tom Swift, Sr.'s top-floor office.

Tom found his father at his desk. Mr. Swift took the wrapping from a flat box and handed it over. "What do you make of this?"

"It was sent by an S. Reisenbach." Tom frowned. "That's the name of the teacher you mentioned last night on that TV interview."

Tom's father nodded. "Ernst Reisenbach was one

of the most brilliant scientists of this century and one of the fathers of nuclear physics. During World War Two, he helped build the first atom bomb. Then Reisenbach was at Princeton for the next twenty years, teaching the next generation of scientists—including me."

He removed a letter from on top of the faded, dusty box in front of him.

" 'Dear Mr. Swift,' " he read aloud. " 'I listened with pride when you mentioned my great-uncle on "Up Front and in Person." We found this box, marked E. Reisenbach, while cleaning out the attic. When my husband and I saw you on TV, we decided that Uncle Ernst would have liked you to have his work.' "

Mr. Swift opened the box, to reveal a pile of yellowed papers covered with intricate math. As Tom's father followed the equations, his eyes grew large. "Reisenbach was years ahead when it came to theoretical physics. Here he postulates that besides the four dimensions we know—length, width, depth, and duration—there are seven other dimensions. These equations are for sending an object back along the space-time axis."

"That's ridiculous," Tom scoffed. "Unless he had a working time machine." He stared for a second, then dashed around his father's desk. "If Professor Reisenbach pulled *that* off, we ought to duplicate his experiments."

Three-thousand miles away in the east coast city of Bayport, Frank and Joe Hardy watched their father shake hands with a wiry man in a drab suit.

"This will be a different sort of case for me, Professor Drake," Fenton Hardy said, smiling. "Usually I trace criminals, not famous physicists."

"And usually I do not require the services of, ahem, private investigators to assist my research." Professor Drake peered over his half-glasses. "Dr. Reisenbach became a bit of a hermit after he left Princeton. His later years are shrouded in, well, mystery."

"How mysterious could a sixty-year-old professor get?" Joe Hardy's blue eyes gleamed impishly as he whispered to his older brother.

Frank Hardy ignored Joe's joking, a serious look on his lean features. "You think there's something mysterious in Dr. Reisenbach's papers?"

The professor shook his bald head. "The mystery is where those papers are." He handed a card to Fenton Hardy. "Here is my phone number. Good luck, and good hunting!" Drake shook hands with the boys and left.

For three days the Hardys banged their heads against a seemingly solid stone wall. "The guy is all over the public record till 1964," Frank complained. "Then he retires from the university, sells his house, cashes in all his investments, and *poof!* he's gone."

"Guys don't go *poof!* from May of one year to November of the next," Joe said.

"I think I can help with that," Fenton Hardy told them. "Dr. Reisenbach had a house in Canada. Technically, he still owns it. How would you like to check it out?"

"We've come pretty far in only two weeks." Tom looked at the mass of equipment that had taken over half of the Swift physics lab. Copies of Reisenbach's original designs were tacked on the walls, sometimes altered or completely revamped.

"It's amazing what he did with sixties technology," Mr. Swift said. "A working model of this thing would have taken up most of a house!"

"By substituting microchips for transistors, we've shrunk it down to manageable size," Tom admitted. "But it seems like a lot of work for a time machine that leaves you stranded in the past."

"We have only hints of that in Reisenbach's notes. Only testing will tell." Mr. Swift powered up the equipment. "Is the test material in place?"

Tom used a pair of tongs to set down a heavy lead bar. "All set, Dad. Is Harlan ready on the other end?"

"He's personally standing guard over his office safe," Mr. Swift said, grinning. "And he's wondering why I'm making him do that, since he knows the safe is empty." The smile faded. "Let's see if we can change that."

Tom joined his father behind a blast shield on the far side of the room. "All circuits are working," Mr. Swift reported, checking a set of gauges. "Energizing."

The hairs at the back of Tom's neck prickled as if an electrical charge had filled the air. He stared as a purplish glow suddenly surrounded the lead bar. "The field is forming," he said.

An indescribable sensation seized Tom, as if his body—or was it the world around him?—were being twisted. Everything went blurry.

Then the bar was gone.

Mr. Swift cut the power, his eyes glowing with excitement. "Let's get over to security," he said.

They reached Harlan's office to find him standing in front of his safe. "Let's see the inside," Mr. Swift said.

"I know what we'll see." The head of Swift Enterprises' security was a bit annoyed as he worked the dial. "Nothing. You made me remove— What the—?"

Harlan Ames whirled to stare at the Swifts. "What's that lead brick doing in there? I've been standing here since I emptied the stupid safe."

The Swifts grinned in triumph. They had sent the ingot back one minute into the past, aiming for the safe's coordinates.

"Don't tell me," Harlan said. "You invented some kind of cockamamie matter transmitter."

Laughing, Tom shook his head. "Even better, Harlan—a time machine."

Two days later, Harlan Ames still looked unhappy as he stared out the windshield of a Swift Enterprises' hovercraft. The all-terrain vehicle had whisked out onto the waters of the Pacific Ocean.

"Today we'll test the time trigger's capability for long-range travel," Mr. Swift told him. "Anchorage Rock is perfect for that purpose. No one has ever lived there, and according to our geological data, it was once considerably more low-lying than it is today."

"Is that why you had the team out there, digging a hole in the ground?" Harlan asked.

"We wanted to bring the time trigger as close as possible to the old level," Tom admitted. "The further back we send the test module, the less accurately we can place it spatially."

He
sent back a
appear in tl
had been a
where the b

"I was a
said. "It's
occupy the
not carefu
they'll blo
efficiency."

Workers
land as the
ticed that
place.

"Oh, no," Tom breathed.
Earth built robots like that.
The minichopper swoop
of fire darted from un
attack rocket!
Tom whirled to
He flung himsel
as the stutter
men!" he
The S
the sa

With the help of the workers and some security people, they unloaded the prototype time machine.

"Set the test module," Mr. Swift said.

Tom swung down into the excavation, carrying a container about a foot long and four inches wide. Tom placed the module in the center of the time trigger, then climbed out of the way. If everything went right, the module would be flung back into the past.

A worried voice cut off their preparations. "Sir! Our sensors—they've gone dead!"

Harlan Ames leapt to the portable radio he'd taken from the hovercraft. "Perimeter guards!" he yelled. "Heads up!"

Even as Ames spoke, Tom heard the *thwip-thwip-thwip* of rotor blades as he ran for cover.

A moment later the helicopter came into view. It looked almost like a scale model, its body barely six feet long. It had to be under remote control. Either that, or the aircraft was a flying robot.

." Only one man on
The Black Dragon!

d into a curve, and a lance
der its stabilizing wings. An

see a figure rising from the water.
to take down his father and Harlan
of automatic gunfire filled the air. "Frog-
yelled.
wift workers and security guards dropped to
nds. Many of them, though, didn't move.
We're being massacred," Harlan said tightly.
Run for the hovercraft!"

Tom ran across the sands, his father right beside him. Two guards joined them, firing as they ran. Only one made it to the hovercraft.

Mr. Swift dove into the vehicle and started the engines. The hovercraft lifted off the ground on roaring fans. Harlan jumped aboard, and Mr. Swift piloted them away from the island.

Harlan stared back at the beach and the still figures there. "What about the ones who didn't make it?" he asked.

Either they're dead, or they've fallen into the hands of the Black Dragon." Mr. Swift's voice was bleak. "And so has the prototype time trigger."

Frank and Joe Hardy drove a rental car out of the Niagara Falls airport, heading for the Canadian side of the border.

They turned onto a small dirt path that wound under a canopy of dripping pine trees. The trees opened out into a small clearing, where a comfortably

old-fashioned log cabin stood. It looked r̶
rain and was obviously not lived in.

Frank opened the car door. "There doesn̶
to be anybody around." He stepped over to the r̶
window and peered in.

"But someone has been here," Joe said in a puzzled voice. He pointed at the damp ground in front
of the cabin door. Frank saw footprints, tracks of a
pair of stout boots heading away from the house.

"Well, he's gone now." Frank stood in the driz-
zling rain, an uneasy feeling in the pit of his stomach.
"I think we should try to find the person who made
those footprints. I'll get the car," he said.

They stopped at a gas station for a fill-up and
some information. "Has anybody come through
here lately?" Frank asked.

The young gas jockey thought for a second. "A
guy in a blue pickup. Had this geezer riding along.
He paid." The gas jockey laughed. "You should have
seen his face when he saw what it cost."

"Can you give us a description?" Frank asked.

The gas jockey shrugged. "Old. Bald. White hair.
Skin and bones."

"Did you notice which way the truck went?" Joe
asked.

The gas jockey pointed toward town. "I heard the
geezer say something about going to the library."

Frank looked at Joe. "What do you say we catch
up on our reading?"

When they arrived at the library, they found a thin
crowd, mainly older people stopping by for a look at
the newspaper. One member of the sparse crowd,
however, had no interest in current affairs. He sat in
a corner, surrounded by encyclopedias, yearbooks,

almanacs, and coffee-table books on the sixties, seventies, eighties, and nineties.

The man put a book down, and Frank stepped back, staggering. That weird feeling was back in the pit of his stomach, backed up with a chill down his spine.

He'd seen that face before, in books on the history of science.

The man was Ernst Reisenbach.

For days the Hardys and Dr. Reisenbach zigzagged across the country, surviving two encounters with the Black Dragon's robot attack force. Now, on a ridge overlooking Swift Enterprises, they had caught up with Tom Swift.

Tom stared at the older man, then declared to the Hardys, "That guy has to be a phony. The real Reisenbach disappeared thirty years ago. He'd be over ninety today."

"There are ways to hop over thirty years," Reisenbach said. He calmly ran a hand over the components of the time machine Tom had set up. "I am amazed at how *compact* you have made my apparatus. Miniaturization technology has certainly progressed since 1965."

Tom's mouth hung open for a second. Then he managed to say, "You—you mean to say you've created a machine that goes *forward* in time? All we've been able to construct is a machine that goes into the past."

"Ah," Reisenbach said. "I believe I know which papers fell into your hands, then. They only represented earlier stages of my work."

"Listen, we need to track down a time trigger,"

Tom said. "One was stolen by the Black Dragon—Xavier Mace. I've seen Mace pervert scientific discoveries into weapons of terror. Who knows what he'll do with a time machine?"

Harlan Ames was at the front gate when Tom and the others arrived at the Swift Enterprises complex.

"What was the big idea of going out alone?" Ames demanded, his face going red under his leathery tan. "We're supposed to be under full security, and you pull a fool stunt like that. Something's happened, and your father has been searching all over for you."

He glanced at the rental car. "And who are those people?"

"They're here to help," Tom said. "I'd better take them straight to Dad."

He whisked them straight to the administration building, and up the elevator to the top-floor office of Tom Swift, Sr. His father sat frowning behind his desk. "I hope you have—"

His voice ran out as he stared at Professor Reisenbach, standing behind Tom with the Hardys.

"Professor! Sir!" Tom senior was out from behind his desk, hurrying over to shake hands with Reisenbach. "How could you— Oh. You figured out how to come forward, too."

Reisenbach nodded, looking out the window and around the grounds of the Swift complex. "I congratulate you on how far you've come since your student days." Then a cloud passed over his features. "Now tell me about Xavier Mace."

Tom senior's face went grim. "I expect my son has told you that Mace succeeded in stealing our copy of your time machine." Reisenbach nodded, and Tom's father breathed a long sigh. "Now he's decided to use it, and the government has turned to me for help. Earlier this afternoon a metal box suddenly appeared from nowhere on the president's desk in the Oval Office. It simply materialized in a glow of purple light."

"The guy knows how to make an impression," Joe Hardy whispered to his brother.

"Inside the box was a videotape. Watch." Mr. Swift tapped a button. Immediately the wall opposite the desk began to glow as a floor-to-ceiling image appeared.

It was a man's face, with well-cut dark hair going gray, steady gray eyes, and slightly chubby cheeks that seemed chubbier as the man smiled.

Tom Swift recognized the face immediately as one of the many masks of the Black Dragon.

The image on the wall continued to smile. "Mr. President," Mace said in a pleasant voice. "As I'm sure you'll agree by the way this tape has appeared on your desk, I have developed an entirely new delivery system, for messages—"

Mace's smile disappeared. "Or weapons. I assure you, sir, that no amount of missile research or Star Wars technology can protect against it. My delivery system is a time machine."

For a second, a sneer passed over Mace's face, then he went on. "My proposal is simple. You are now the leader of the only superpower on Earth. Henceforth, you will confer with me on all policy matters, and I will have the final say. The world need never know." Mace's eyes went flat and ugly for a moment.

"You have one week to consider my proposal. If

you accept, merely arrange a press conference and use the words, 'A wise leader takes advisement from all quarters.' " Xavier Mace smiled. "I will then arrange for regular communication."

Then the smile faded, and the face looking out from the wall was hard and unyielding. "If after a week you have not agreed, I shall have to give a more potent demonstration of my abilities. A more public demonstration, too."

Mace leaned forward, his eyes icy cold. "Somewhere in America a city will be destroyed—completely and utterly."

Want more?
Read the complete exciting story in

TIME BOMB

A Hardy Boys and Tom Swift Ultra Thriller™
Available July 15, 1992
Wherever Paperbacks Are Sold